"I'm A Tarkent[...] With [...]"

"You won't get away with Katie. I'll take her to the ends of the earth to keep her away from you, Jack."

"I'm one of the privileged few who has the resources to follow you there. You won't be able to hide her, not from me. I have too much money and too many connections. And when I do find her, I'll use your refusal to acknowledge me as her father against you, not only in a court of law, but in the court of public opinion."

"You want to ruin her life by making this public? Is that it?"

"I'm her father. I am not going to go away. I laid out my proposal. You can either turn this into a public custody battle or marry me and keep Katie's paternity private. Unlike you, I believe both her parents have Katie's best interests at heart."

Dear Reader,

This May we invite you to delve into six delicious new titles from Silhouette Desire!

We begin with the brand-new title you've been eagerly awaiting from the incomparable Ann Major. *Love Me True,* our May MAN OF THE MONTH, is a riveting reunion romance offering the high drama and glamour that are Ann's hallmarks.

The enjoyment continues in FORTUNE'S CHILDREN: THE BRIDES with *The Groom's Revenge* by Susan Crosby. A young working woman is swept off her feet by a wealthy CEO who's married her with more than love on his mind—he wants revenge on the father who never claimed her, Stuart Fortune. A "must read" for all you fans of Daphne Du Maurier's *Rebecca!*

Barbara McMahon's moving story *The Cowboy and the Virgin* portrays the awakening—both sensual and emotional—of an innocent young woman who falls for a ranching Romeo. But can she turn the tables and corral *him?* Beverly Barton's emotional miniseries 3 BABIES FOR 3 BROTHERS concludes with *Having His Baby.* Experience the birth of a father as well as a child when a rugged rancher is transformed by the discovery of his secret baby—and the influence of her pretty mom. Then, in her exotic SONS OF THE DESERT title, *The Solitary Sheikh,* Alexandra Sellers depicts a hard-hearted sheikh who finds happiness with his daughters' aristocratic tutor. And *The Billionaire's Secret Baby* by Carol Devine is a compelling marriage-of-convenience story.

Now more than ever, Silhouette Desire offers you the most passionate, powerful and provocative of sensual romances. Make yourself merry this May with all six Desire novels—and buy another set for your mom or a close friend for Mother's Day!

Enjoy!

Joan Marlow Golan
Senior Editor, Silhouette Desire

Please address questions and book requests to:
Silhouette Reader Service
U.S.: 3010 Walden Ave., P.O. Box 1325, Buffalo, NY 14269
Canadian: P.O. Box 609, Fort Erie, Ont. L2A 5X3

THE BILLIONAIRE'S
SECRET BABY
CAROL DEVINE

SILHOUETTE *Desire*®
Published by Silhouette Books
America's Publisher of Contemporary Romance

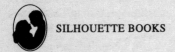 SILHOUETTE BOOKS

ISBN 0-373-76218-6

THE BILLIONAIRE'S SECRET BABY

Books by Carol Devine

Silhouette Desire

Beauty and the Beastmaster #816
A Man of the Land #909
The Billionaire's Secret Baby #1218

CAROL DEVINE

lives in Colorado with her husband and three sons, including identical twins. When she's not playing pick-up games of basketball and hunting for lost Reeboks, she's holed up in her office, dreaming of romantic heroes.

Her writing has won numerous awards, including the Romance Writers of America's 1992 Golden Heart for Short Contemporary Series Romance. She has also served as president of Rocky Mountain Fiction Writers.

One

Meg Masterson Betz couldn't believe it. The father of her child had dared come to her husband's funeral.

Jack Tarkenton edged the crowd of mourners, standing a little apart, larger than life, richer than rich, his signature mane of lion-colored hair stirring in the fall breeze. Powerfully built and conservatively dressed, he looked so much like his late, great father, Meg recognized him instantly.

She wasn't the only one. Near the line of limousines parked along the cemetery road, the paparazzi and media types had mobilized and were madly taking pictures of the latest Tarkenton arrival.

Grateful for the black veil concealing her face, Meg made sure she had a firm grip on her daughter's hand. Katie was behaving extremely well for a four-year-old, but the last thing she needed was a dozen cameras in her face.

Unfortunately, that was the price of being related to the famous Tarkenton family, even if only by marriage. Like the Kennedys, the Tarkentons attracted attention wherever they went. And Jack, as his late father's only son, namesake and heir apparent, was the most famous Tarkenton of them all.

Double-breasted Armani boxed his shoulders with the clean and proper lines of the classiest in charcoal wool suits. A pristine shirt and maroon tie echoed this concession to convention.

Really, Meg thought. The briefest in beach attire was more his thing. Apparently, Jack wasn't slumming today.

A pair of sunglasses cut the bronzed boldness of his well-known face in two. That disturbed her, to have him this close and not be able to see his eyes. The uncompromising set of his jaw, however, made her remember the aggressive self-assurance behind the sunglasses all too well.

Why was he here? He hadn't known Allen. He certainly didn't know her. Not really. The only connection she had to John B. Tarkenton Jr. was her brother's marriage to his sister. That marriage and her child.

His child.

Meg flinched at the thought. Sometimes she hated her penchant for honesty. It cut like a knife to remember how stupid she had been. When Allen offered to marry her and raise the child as his own, holding back the truth was a discipline she had to constantly work at to maintain. Having a kind and decent husband like Allen helped, but Katie was the one who made her strong. That's what came from having children.

You have a God-given chance to make things right, even when you started wrong.

Meg glanced at her daughter's dark head. The coffee-brown curls matched her own. Katie's brown eyes matched her father's, however, and that was the one truth Meg would carry to her grave as Allen had carried it to his. Steadfast and loyal, he'd been Katie's father in every way that mattered. Thanks to him, Jack Tarkenton would never know he had even fathered a child. He wasn't going to get a chance to corrupt her little girl.

Shuddering, Meg turned her attention to the minister as he delivered the final prayer. By prearranged signal, he spread his arms wide and spoke to the entire assemblage. "And now the widow and daughter of Allen Betz would like a private moment. If you would kindly exit to the left, the burial site will be opened to the public in a few minutes' time."

Meg squeezed Katie's hand. "You ready, sweetie? It's time."

Katie looked up with her big brown eyes and nodded, her long, dark curls glinting in the late-morning sun. Such a pretty child. Such a solemn child. Allen's death had hit her hard.

Meg led the way past the mourners spilling out onto the lawn and halted at the casket. Kneeling, she placed her hand on the polished wood surface and bowed her head. Katie imitated every move.

The sight of the small hand on the polished wood brought a lump to Meg's throat. All her instincts, maternal and otherwise, told her this was the right thing to do. Katie needed to grieve. But that was poor comfort to a mother's desire to shield her child's heart.

Meg thought of Allen, gentle Allen, and her sorrow twisted into a strange type of guilt. In the three days since the car accident that took his life, she had yet to shed a tear. All she knew was that she should have loved him better. She should have loved him more.

The click and whir of cameras—present only because of the Tarkentons—made her grief feel less than real, like it was put on for show. Meg put a shielding arm around Katie and pulled her close. Was nothing sacred anymore? The last thing either of them needed was to be the subject of prying eyes.

Upset with the photographers, with Jack, with herself, Meg helped Katie to her feet. Together they walked to the minister, and Meg thanked him for the service. Katie echoed the sentiment by silently offering to shake the elderly man's hand.

"God bless and keep you, child," he said.

Katie's newest aunt, Sarah Masterson, came forward next. Despite her maternity dress and the swell of her belly, she held out her arms, her heartfelt hug steadying Meg. Sarah then knelt and offered her arms to Katie.

Katie walked right into them, taking to her new aunt like a fish to water, much as her Uncle Zach had done. Meg accepted his hug with gratitude, finding solace in his down-to-earth rancher's strength. "You okay?" he asked, placing his black cowboy hat on his head.

Meg nodded to relieve the worry in his sky blue eyes. "Thank you for flying all the way to New Jersey from Wyoming, Zach. It means more than I can say. And to have Sarah here, too. I've never seen Katie accept anybody so readily."

"Sarah and I thought we'd take Katie off your hands for a while. There's a duck pond over yonder, in the middle of the cemetery grounds."

"Yes, by all means. Please make sure she stays away from the photographers."

"Will do." He touched the brim of his hat, then knelt next to his wife and tweaked Katie's nose. "Hey, bright eyes. Your Aunt Sarah and I are going to check out the ducks. Want to come?"

Katie nodded with her usual gravity. Zach scooped her up, setting her burgundy dress swinging like a bell. Meg mouthed a thank-you to Sarah and the three of them set off together, creating a picture of what was to come in a few months' time when Zach and Sarah had a child of their own.

Allen had wanted a child of his own, too.

Meg hid her distress at the thought and turned to greet the other mourners. She pressed their hands in sincerity, moved to speak personally to the many who had come. She even managed a smile when her oldest brother, Bram, slipped a strong and supportive arm around her waist. "You holding up?"

"I'm fine."

"Now, Meg, tell the truth." Amanda, Bram's blond wife, touched Meg's hand. "This is your big brother, remember? The Master of all Mastersons. You can tell him anything."

Hesitating, Meg sighed. "The truth is, I am a little worn. But that's to be expected, isn't it?"

Amanda murmured in sympathy and pressed Meg's hand. The circle of family widened as Meg was embraced by her other brother, Joe, and her sister, Elizabeth. Last came her mother, Mary Masterson, who pressed fresh tissues into Meg's hands. "Can I do anything else for you, honey?"

"You're doing it, Mama." Meg reached to bring the entire family into a shared embrace. "You're all doing it."

Elizabeth smiled through her freely flowing tears. "Hey, I'm the big sister here. I'm the one who is supposed to be bucking you up."

"But you are." Meg gave Elizabeth a squeeze. But Meg's gaze inevitably strayed to Katie, safe with Sarah and Zach at the pond.

"Hard to believe our baby brother is going to be a father soon," Bram commented.

"I know," Meg replied, relieved at the change of subject. "I thought he would be the last to settle down. But once I met Sarah and saw how special she is, I began to understand."

"I hear she's been his saving grace."

Meg startled at the distinctive, deep voice of Jack Tarkenton. To her dismay, he joined the family throng as though he belonged. To see him casually appraising her, sans sunglasses, caused Meg to shrink inside.

The personal nature of his comment startled everyone else as well. Even his sister Amanda appeared taken aback. "Jack, I didn't realize you even knew who Sarah and Zach were."

"It would be difficult to miss the newest member of the Masterson family. Zach ought to be congratulated on his good taste."

"I wouldn't congratulate him too much if I were you, Jack," Bram warned. "He knows your reputation with the ladies."

"Speaking of ladies..." Jack offered a handshake

to Meg. "I wanted to express my sincere sympathy for your loss. I know it's a cliché, but if there is anything I can do to help you or your daughter, please don't hesitate to call."

Aware of the clicking cameras, Meg steeled herself and took the hand. He pressed a card into her palm, a business card, of all things. As though he had a real business.

Meg knew she was supposed to politely nod and thank him. Instead, she crumpled the card in her fist and reached for Bram's arm, leaning on his big build and brawn. "I think it's time for Katie and I to go home."

Jack Tarkenton was easy to avoid after that. The limousine was reserved for immediate family only. When he showed up at her house later that afternoon after she started receiving guests, Meg announced she and Katie needed to go upstairs and rest for a while. Even someone as callous as Jack Tarkenton couldn't argue with that.

She figured wrong, however. He intercepted her at the base of the stairs. "When you're free, I'd like a moment with you—alone."

Speechless at his gall, she fled up the stairs with Katie in her arms. When Meg gained the landing, she stared down at him, letting her disapproval show. But he continued to follow her with those eyes, gleaming brown as the finest dark chocolate.

Katie's eyes.

Hugging her daughter close, Meg hurried into Katie's room and locked the door behind them. "It's nap time, sweetheart."

"But I don't want to take a nap."

"Of course you don't," Meg soothed, setting her

down on the edge of her pink ruffled bed. "But we'll change your clothes, anyway. You don't want to get wrinkles all over your pretty dress."

"It's Daddy's favorite."

"I know." Meg undid the buckles on Katie's patent leather shoes and slipped them off. "I'm sure he was glad to see you wear it today."

"Mommy, when can I go to heaven to see Daddy?"

Meg drew Katie's dress off, feeling how hard this was going to be on both her and her daughter. "You miss him already, don't you?"

She nodded, and her large eyes pooled with tears. "I want my daddy."

"Oh, baby, I know." Meg kissed the top of Katie's head and helped her change into her pajamas. "I wish he was here, too."

"You do?"

"Oh, yes. He was a wonderful daddy, a wonderful daddy to us both."

"When can I see him?"

Meg gave her the plush toy rabbit she always slept with and picked up Allen's framed photograph on the nightstand. "Remember what I told you this morning? Daddy's picture will stay right beside your bed. Then you can see him whenever you want."

"Forever?"

"Forever."

Meg helped Katie set the picture safely on the nightstand. Clutching her rabbit, she lay down and stared at Allen's picture with such studious concentration, it broke Meg's heart. "Mommy, can I have the light on? I want Daddy to see me."

"I'll leave the light on, and the light in the bathroom, too. If you get scared or need anything, you call me, okay?''

"Okay." Katie opened her arms for a hug. "I love you, Mommy."

"I love you, too, sweetheart. Daddy does, too."

Meg tucked the covers around Katie and kissed her forehead. "Sleep tight."

"Don't let the bedbugs bite."

Exiting swiftly, Meg drew the door closed to the point where she could still hear any sounds in the room, if need be. Standing in the hall, she wiped her eyes and listened the way all mothers listened, to make sure her child was settling down.

How many times had she done this? How many times had she kissed Katie good-night? Hundreds of times. And how many times had she kissed Allen good-night?

Hardly ever.

"Is she asleep?"

Jumping, Meg spotted Jack Tarkenton's broad-shouldered silhouette standing in the shadows at the end of the hall. "I need to talk to you," he said, his voice hushed. "Now."

She advanced on him, using her most forceful whisper. "I think I've made it abundantly clear that I have no desire whatsoever to talk with you." She stabbed a finger at the stairs. "Please leave."

"Don't make this harder than it already is, Meg. I only want a few minutes of your time."

"How dare you," she whispered furiously. "How dare you come to my husband's funeral. How dare you come to my house. How dare you come any-where near me."

"Katie's mine, Meg. I know it and you know it,

so stop the righteous-sounding speech and take me to someplace private where we can talk.''

Meg stared at him, seeing his coldness while feeling her own anger drain into the well of her deepest fear. No, this could not be happening. He could not have said—

''You heard me. I know I'm Katie's father.''

''No,'' she breathed. ''You're not.''

''I was there when she was conceived, remember?''

She pushed past him. '' 'Remember' is the last thing I want to do, especially with my husband barely cold in his grave. He's Katie's father. Not you.''

Jack caught her arm. ''I'm warning you, Meg. There are plenty of people downstairs. We can do this in private or we can do this in public. It makes no difference to me.''

She wrenched her arm from him. ''Get away from me.''

''Not until you hear me out.''

''No.'' She ducked to make her voice heard on the level below. ''Bram?''

''Yeah?''

''I need you upstairs.''

''I'll be right there, Meg.''

Triumphant, she turned to find Jack leaning against the wall, hands slung in the trouser pockets of his impeccable suit. ''Big brother doesn't know about us, does he? If he knew, my sister would know, and she would have come straight to me. I wonder how Bram and Amanda will feel when the two of them find out precisely what we were doing on the sacred occasion of their wedding day.''

"Amanda's your sister. You wouldn't do that to her."

"Try me."

Meg heard Bram's tread on the stairs. "Meg?"

"Here," she called, wishing she could rip the smugness off Jack's face. Or have Bram rip it off.

"Hey, Jack," he greeted. "I didn't know you were up here, too." Bram turned to her. "Meg, what can I do for you?"

Jack's challenging look of inquiry told Meg he wasn't about to retrieve the gauntlet he'd thrown down. She checked her brother's strong, familiar face. All she had to do was tell him the truth. He would forgive her. So would the rest of her family.

The truth shall set you free.

Except where Jack Tarkenton was involved. With his wealth and name, the only thing the truth would set free was a battalion of lawyers. She wasn't ready to have that happen, not yet. Not unless it was the only way to protect Katie.

"I'm sorry, Bram," she said. "Jack heard me call and came up himself."

"Katie just needed an extra good-night kiss," Jack explained, straightening, rising to the occasion with impressive ease. "I'm not her uncle like you, Bram, but considering the circumstances, I thought it was a good sign that Katie was willing to accept one from me."

Chills raced down Meg's spine. She had forgotten how well he lied. She'd also forgotten how incredibly breathless she got when he flashed that celebrated smile of his.

Bram responded to it, too. "It's good to see you here, Jack. It meant a lot to Amanda to have you at the burial service. Meg, too, I'm sure. The more a family comes together in times of crisis, the stronger it will be.''

Sickened by the irony in that little speech, Meg plunged down the stairs between them. What family? With Allen dead at the hands of a drunk driver, hers was destroyed. Now she had to deal with Jack Tarkenton. How in the world had he found out the truth? Other than to Allen, she had never breathed her secret to anyone.

Thankfully, the only mourners who lingered downstairs were members of her own family. Gathered on the backyard patio, they were enjoying the warmth of the dying sun while Bram and Amanda's three-year-old son, J.J., played on the swing set.

Meg decided if she was going to have a showdown with Jack, the kitchen was the place to do it. The heart of her house was cozy and filled with the many small touches that made it her own. Herbs grew on the windowsill and copper-bottomed pots hung from a rack above the stove, matching the warm tones of terra cotta and eggnog. More important to Meg, the kitchen overlooked the backyard, within calling distance of her family.

At the approach of male voices, she hid her serious attack of nerves by starting a new pot of coffee and busily laying out fresh cookies on a plate. She addressed her brother when he and Jack entered. ''Bram, would you let everyone know out back there's more coffee on the way?''

''Sure. I wanted to check on Amanda and J.J., anyway.'' Bram pecked her cheek and stole one of the cookies as he headed for the door. ''Keep Meg company, will you, Jack?''

"What's a brother-in-law for?"

The moment the door closed, Meg folded her arms and turned on him. "I want to know why you think you're Katie's father."

"I don't think—I know. I had you followed."

"Followed! When?"

"After our passionate weekend," he replied, helping himself to coffee. "All the women I sleep with have to pass muster, you see. I use the services of a private investigator, an extremely discreet one, I might add. Saves me from some nasty surprises. Like yours, for example."

"Katie was not a nasty surprise."

"Your marriage was." He sipped from his mug, inspecting her with interest as he lounged against the counter, completely relaxed in his thousand dollar suit and hundred dollar tie.

Meg hid the tremor of her hands by wrapping them around her mug. "You must have heard about it. I asked Amanda to tell your side of the family."

"She did, a week or so after the fact. Amanda also mentioned it wasn't like you to be so secretive, Meg. All of a sudden you up and eloped, without one word to anybody. It created quite a stir, even in my family."

"It shouldn't have. Allen and I had known each other since childhood."

"Yes, I understand he lived in the same neighborhood when you were kids. My investigator informed me, however, that the two of you lost touch with each other soon after you won that scholarship to the Sorbonne and moved away. Any truth to the rumor that good old Allen showed up on your doorstep at the precise moment you most needed a man to marry?''

"How can you say that? He was my husband. I loved him.''

"The question is, did you love him before you found out you were pregnant or after? My sources tell me he came into the picture *after* your positive pregnancy test. Several weeks after, in fact.''

He did know everything. Stunned, Meg braced herself against the kitchen counter. Through the window above the sink, she saw the tree Allen had planted in the backyard the day Katie was born. "What do you want?''

"Katie.''

Meg stared at him. "You must be out of your mind.''

"I don't think a judge will think so, not in this day and age. Not when the rights of both biological parents are considered more or less equally. And since my daughter has been deliberately kept from me by her mother for almost five years, the judge may give my custody petition special consideration. Who knows what might happen?''

"If you wanted Katie so much, you should have come forward long before now.''

"And break up your little family? I'm much too noble for that. But now that Allen is gone...'' Jack let the sentence hang, then smiled in cynical fashion. "Everybody in the country knows I lost my father at an early age. How can I allow my own flesh and blood to grow up without a father, too? What do you think, Meg? Will the tabloids buy it?''

"You're despicable.''

He chuckled. "I think it makes pretty good copy

myself. Might even score a special on TV. You know how famous we Tarkentons are."

"You think this is funny? You think you can come in here and destroy my daughter's life?"

"I'm not here to destroy anything. I want to be a father to Katie."

"Over my dead body."

He eyed her over the rim of his mug, amused. "Meg, I'd forgotten your flair for the dramatic."

"I am not being dramatic. Unlike you, I *mean* what I say."

"Oh, I get it. The woman scorned. You believed me when I said I'd call you."

Meg pointed at the door. "Get out. Get out of my house."

He became deadly serious, zeroing in on her with an intensity of purpose she recalled all too well. "You're right. This is neither the time nor place to make a grieving widow relive her past. Believe it or not, I thought long and hard about whether I should force myself on you today. But there may be another Allen waiting in the wings. You surprised me once, Meg. You won't surprise me again. I want to know my daughter."

"Do you have any idea what this will do to her?"

"I'm fully aware I don't know Katie as well as you do. That's why I need your help."

"Oh, please. Do you think I'd actually help you? Do you really think I'd let someone like you anywhere near my daughter?"

"Our daughter, Meg," he said gently.

"No! She's mine, mine and Allen's. He's the only father she has ever known. I won't let you take her away from me."

"I don't want to take her, not from you. You're all she's got. I know it and you know it. That's your ace in the hole and you can bet it's a winning card. The last thing I would do to her, or to you, too, is take her away from you."

"I know you, Jack. Everybody does. You use people. I wouldn't trust you no matter what you said."

"That's the beauty of my plan. You don't have to trust me."

"If that's supposed to ease my mind, you're sadly mistaken. In fact, I'm not interested in anything you have to say." She headed for the door.

"You'd better be interested." He blocked her way.

The quickness of his move flashed a memory of his body, lithe and naked, blocking her way. Except she'd liked it then. It meant he hadn't wanted her to leave, and she'd allowed him to catch her and kiss her and carry her back to his bed. The memory heated her body as surely as it froze her soul. How could she? How could she have done that with him?

"Katie will be protected at all costs," he said. "You can't tell me that doesn't matter to you."

She backed away from him. "I will not let you use me to get to my daughter."

"I'll sweeten the deal. Out of the goodness of my heart, Allen retains his official title as father. You won't have to break the news to Katie or anyone else that I'm her real father. It can be our little secret."

Unable to tear herself away from what she saw in his eyes, half promise and half challenge, Meg felt the solidity of the kitchen counter against her spine. "I'm listening."

"I can see that. But you know me, Meg. I need

complete capitulation. I need to hear you tell me you're ready and willing to hear me out.''

It was so like him to do this, to force her to bend to his will. Meg couldn't believe she once let this man get close enough to burn her heart. She jerked a chair out from the kitchen table and, seating herself, wrapped her hands protectively around her coffee mug. ''Well?''

He chuckled. ''Before we start, how about a refill on the coffee? You look like you could use one.''

He refreshed their mugs, and she couldn't help but notice his hands, long-fingered and well tanned, and the image rose of how dark they had once looked on her skin. Her most intimate skin.

She gulped the coffee, hoping to sear some sense into herself. The steaming liquid burned her tongue, her throat, burned all the way down, and still the mere sight of his hands caused the warmth to spread, the warmth and wetness that kept her immobile and ashamed. How could this be happening? How could she be physically attracted to this morally bankrupt man?

He took the chair opposite her and reached for her hand. She refused to give it, keeping stubborn hold of her mug.

He peeled her fingers away one by one, and she let him, God help her, she let him, for more memories sprang to life, memories of Allen doing the exact same thing once, the day she was at her most desperate, the day he asked her to marry him.

Except Allen's hands had been stubby, tentative and damp. And she hadn't been gripping her mug as much as playing with it, using it as ballast, as a focal point, as she spilled her tale of woe to the boy she once knew as Al-the-pal Betz.

And the overeager and earnest sheen of Allen's eyes would have been lost on Jack, lost in the darkness of his soul. For he was after her daughter, claiming to care, claiming to know. As he once claimed her.

Allen had not been able to break that claim, despite his kind and generous heart. The only thing Allen claimed was that he wanted to help her, if only she would let him. He claimed she didn't have to confess the shame of her pregnancy or name the baby's father to another living soul. He would be the baby's father. He would raise it as his own. Say yes to his proposal, he told her, and she would make him the happiest of men. That's when Allen got down on his knees and begged her to marry him.

Jack Tarkenton wasn't one to beg, however. He had gone on his knees before her, though, the first time they made love. He'd kissed her and stripped her and knelt at her feet, and she was haunted by needs she never knew she had. Jack satisfied every one of them, leaving her lost to Allen, lost to any other man.

Even now, Jack dared her with his wicked smile, the smile that once enticed her to be wicked, too, and guilt billowed inside her. Guilt chased by a terrible drenching of shame.

For if he proposed what Allen had, if Jack asked her to be his wife, Meg wanted, in her heart of hearts, she wanted, to her great and everlasting shame, to say *yes*.

Two

The day had taken its toll.

Subtle blue bruised Meg's skin, especially under the eyes, those ocean blue eyes Jack had worked long and hard to forget. The ebony of her dress brought out the depth of their color, as did the mahogany frame of her hair.

Even in deepest mourning, she radiated an ethereal beauty. It showed in the elegance of her bearing, in the finely wrought bones of her face. Her milky skin heightened the bold contrasts in her coloring, emphasizing the lush rose of her lips set against the cool white of her smile.

Except she wasn't smiling. And once he got through with her tonight, she wouldn't be smiling for a long time to come.

Jack crushed the prickling of his conscience, the conscience he thought he'd lost on his first go-round with the lovely Meg Masterson. But her beauty had blossomed in the five years since he had last seen her, when she'd been fresh-faced, and willowy of body, packaged in a style and sophistication that came directly from Paris, France.

Later he learned that she had studied art there, and was as poor as she was proud. But when they first met, all he knew was that he must have her, and he targeted her like a hunter would, swift of speed and hard of heart.

And he did have her, that very night. Despite the family and festivities that surrounded them, she allowed him to woo her and lure her, until he spirited her to his hotel room where she stayed with him until dawn. He seduced her the next night, and the next, breaking his most cardinal of rules to not get too involved with any woman. Nobody on this earth had a right to expect a thing from John B. Tarkenton Jr.

Jack reached inside his jacket and pulled out the black velvet ring box. The sight of it made Meg feel something, that much was certain, but the expressive narrowing of her eyes told him it was anger more than anything else.

He couldn't blame her. He'd done plenty of underhanded things in his life, but proposing marriage to his intended on the day of her husband's funeral topped the list. Yet it couldn't be helped. He'd wasted enough time as it was.

He opened the box, revealing the diamond solitaire ring inside. To her credit, her gaze never faltered, never even dropped to see what he offered.

"A gift," he said, placing the open box on the table between them.

"No, it's not. It's a bribe. You want me to marry you."

Baldly stated like that, he wanted to throw up his hands and say, *Hey babe, you got it all wrong.* But she wasn't wrong. Meg had done more than grow up. "I'm impressed," he admitted. "You took the words right out of my mouth. Does that mean you approve?"

"I wouldn't marry you if you were the last man on earth."

It stung. Not much, but enough to put him into attack mode. He left the box in the middle of the table and lounged back in his chair. "You do realize what the alternative is."

"You take me to court and sue for custody of Katie? Given your reputation, that's a chance I'm willing to take."

"Ah, yes. The familiar ground of my reputation." He gave her his laziest smile. "I'm a Tarkenton, Meg. Do you have any idea what that means?"

"It means you were born with a silver spoon in your mouth. It means that despite the best education money can buy, you waste your time on wine, women and song. It means you think so little of your family's good name, you bring heartache to your mother and your sister, the only two people on earth who could possibly care about someone as selfish as you. That's what it means."

He'd learned to shrug off such gibes. He had also acquired the correlated ability to ride roughshod over people. "It means, dear Meg, that when people look at me, they see my father. They want to believe I'm him. They want to believe it so badly, that no matter what I say or what I do, they think I'm the one to lead them to the promised land. You know what being John B. Tarkenton Jr. means? I get away with everything.''

"You won't get away with Katie. I'll take her to the ends of the earth to keep her away from you.''

"I'm one of the privileged few who has the resources to follow you there. You won't be able to hide her, not from me. I have too much money and too many connections. There are Tarkenton interests all over the world. And when I do find her, I'll use your refusal to acknowledge me as her father against you, not only in a court of law, but in the court of public opinion. Don't forget, Meg. My name and face are recognized around the world. Which brings me to the most pertinent fact, a fact you seem to have forgotten. My being a Tarkenton means Katie is a Tarkenton, too.''

"You want to ruin her life by making this public? Is that it?''

"I'm her father. It's a statement of fact. I am not going to go away. I laid out my proposal. You have two weeks to come up with a better one. If you don't, your choice is simple. You can either turn this into a public custody battle or marry me and keep Katie's paternity private, just between us. As her mother, I happen to think you are the most qualified person to make this decision. Unlike you, I believe both her parents have Katie's best interests at heart.''

He shoved the box at her, and then he was gone from her house.

The moment Meg pushed open the thick glass-and-brass doors of New York City's poshest and most exclusive athletic club, she realized she had made a mistake. It was one thing to show up without an appointment at Jack's Wall Street office. It was quite another to confront him here, far from the trappings of executives and professionals.

Her smart navy business suit clashed with the fluorescent glare and neon graphics of the club. Behind a metallic reception desk stood a cute and bouncy girl who wore a brilliant green polo shirt with the club's insignia stitched above her name. "May I help you?" she asked brightly.

Debbie's short sleeves showed off muscular biceps and veins that bulged on her forearms. Intimidating arms they were, too, especially to a woman who was in a crisply tailored jacket, slim skirt and the highest of heels. "Do you happen to know where I can find Jack Tarkenton?" she asked.

Debbie's bright smile disappeared. "I'm sorry. I'm not allowed to give out the names or whereabouts of our members."

Meg tucked her purse under her arm and approached the desk. "What do you do in case of emergencies?"

"Is this an emergency?"

"It is urgent that I speak to Mr. Tarkenton, yes."

Debbie put her hands on formidably narrow hips. "You would not *believe* how many women come in here claiming they know him. I'm sorry, but I'm not allowed to even confirm the fact that he's here."

"I know he's here. I'm his secretary. It is urgent that I speak to him as soon as possible."

"If you're his secretary, why didn't you just call him direct?"

It figured with Jack's active social life, he'd carry a cell phone. "This matter is a rather delicate one,"

Meg explained, hoping the conversation wasn't being monitored. "It really would be best if I talked to him face-to-face."

"One of *those* matters, huh?" Debbie gestured Meg closer. "I've heard he has a bedroom suite in his office. Mirrors, waterbed, hot tub, screening room, the works. True?"

Meg wouldn't be surprised if it was. Before coming here, she went to the address on his business card. It led to a modern office building—gray with granite and sleek with reflecting glass.

However, the pepper-haired receptionist for Tarkenton, Inc., was far cagier and more protective than this young woman, refusing to either confirm or deny whether Mr. Tarkenton was even in the country. Consequently, Meg hadn't glimpsed anything beyond the reception area.

Tastefully decorated in rich rosewood and brass, it was classic and brooding and lawyerlike. Which fit. Like his sister, Amanda, Jack had followed in his father's footsteps long enough to obtain a law degree.

When Meg failed to track him down at the office, she recalled Amanda mentioning this club as one of her brother's frequent haunts.

"Tell you what," Meg said to Debbie. "I'm not allowed to divulge anything about Mr. Tarkenton, either. But if you let me deliver my message, I'll have him autograph something for you."

"He won't give autographs. He won't even sign our register. See?" Debbie showed a clipboard holding a lined sheet scrawled with names and membership numbers.

"Debbie, I'm his secretary," Meg said dryly. "I can get him to sign anything."

"I better not get into trouble over this."

"You won't," Meg assured her, wondering if she'd ever strung so many lies together in her life. "If there's a problem, I'll explain the situation to your boss myself. After I see Mr. Tarkenton, that is. The sooner he gets this information, the better."

Sighing, Debbie picked up the desk phone and punched a few numbers. "Hi, Ben. Uh, I need to check on Mr. Tarkenton's whereabouts. Do you see him down there?" Pause. "By himself? Okay, thanks." She hung up the phone. "He's in one of our squash courts, practicing. If I let you go down there, you have to promise to come right back after you deliver your message."

"You don't have to worry about that. I have no intention of staying any longer than necessary."

"He didn't get somebody knocked up, did he?"

Even Meg wasn't prepared for that bombshell of a question. Utterly speechless, she blinked in disbelief.

Debbie waved a placating hand. "I know you won't tell me. I've always been curious, though. With all the women he has, you'd think he'd have a kid here or there, you know?"

Meg knew only too well, and fixed Debbie with a genuine glare. The young woman immediately apologized and wrote out a temporary membership card allowing free access to the club.

Shaken, Meg had to use both hands to pick the card up. The worst part was, she would have to get used to it. The man attracted this type of gossip and speculation wherever he went.

Meg glanced at the club doors, wishing there was someplace where the Tarkenton arm didn't reach.

There must be people in the world who hadn't heard of Jack Tarkenton, people who didn't know anything about him.

But people the world over knew of his father. In the thirty-plus years since his death, Senator John B. Tarkenton had attained martyr status. Revered for his ethics and character, he had rallied the nation with his youthful vigor and visionary leadership in a last-minute campaign for the presidency of the United States. The triumph of his election ended before he had a chance to take office, in the tragedy of his assassination.

Jack might be his father's polar opposite in character, but the Tarkenton name still carried enormous weight. In a world hungry for leadership, too many people wanted to believe Jack possessed the same talents and integrity as his father.

Meg knew she couldn't fight a belief, especially when it was cherished by people who most needed it to be true. People who wanted to live with hope in their lives, who wanted to believe in the future. Meg counted herself one of those people. She wanted Katie to be one of them, too.

Meg passed row after shiny row of exercise bikes, rowing machines, treadmills and stair climbers, torturous-looking contraptions all, and decided that ten thirty on a Monday morning was not the peak time to exercise. She imagined the place after work hours, though, jam-packed with bodies. Sweating bodies.

Jack was no exception. She spotted him in a glassed-in box of a court, dressed in sleek bike shorts and a gray T-shirt that was dark at the shoulders with sweat. Lithe as she remembered, he stroked a blur of a ball with a thin-necked racket, thwacking a regular rhythm against a scuffed backboard.

The nearer she came, the more she noticed the maleness of his body. Her steps slowed. His shirt hung loose, shaping the broad width of his shoulders. If anything, he'd gained muscle over the years. The bike shorts banded thighs honed by hard and steady exercise. Confirmed by calf muscles that flexed and flared as he moved from one side of the court to the other, he challenged himself on every shot, stretching to cover the entire court. The clear, see-through walls had to be made of super-durable acrylic. The velocity of the ball he hit would have cracked glass.

Above his left hand, the hand that held the racket, two sweatbands encircled his wrist. *So that's where it came from. Katie was left-handed, too.*

Despite her promise to deliver her message promptly, Meg halted in her tracks and watched for long minutes, her throat too dry for words. She knew next to nothing about the game of squash. She understood pure physical aggression, however, and the advantage a supremely focused individual had over those who were mere mortals.

He never missed.

To the world outside, he projected the image of the rich and idle playboy. The bronzed good looks, the lazy charm that reflected the relaxed savoir faire of a man who had seen and experienced all. In recent years he had even gone on record with the most lurid of tabloids, claiming to have little ambition other than to enjoy life and have fun.

Yet there were many people who discounted those claims, calling them a mandate for the future, honest and modest, like father, like son. Once his days of ''sowing his wild oats'' were over, destiny dictated that John B. Tarkenton Jr. would enter into the world of international politics as his father had. And like any prodigal son returning to his true destiny, he'd be exalted and redeemed.

Everyone knew his background. Everyone knew the tragedy of his father's death. He'd grown up in the media spotlight, shadowed by the specter of what might have been. Even Meg was drawn in by the sheer power he embodied. The swiftness of his feet matched a steadiness of purpose that went beyond the physical. He played to win, win at all costs, and a piece of the puzzle that made up Jack Tarkenton fell into place for Meg, a piece that had, before this moment, put terror in her heart.

She had thought he wanted to punish her for some reason, using their daughter as bait. But that was too predictable a strategy for such a fierce competitor. Jack wouldn't waste his time unless he cared about Katie, cared on some level. Which meant he did have a weakness, as the perky gossip Debbie so aptly demonstrated. Nobody in their right mind would think him an appropriate role model for a child, especially a four-year-old girl who had just lost the only father she had ever known. Jack might have plenty of friends in high places and the money to use them, but two could play the game of the media.

Rejuvenated, Meg rapped on the Plexiglas door. Caught in mid-swing, he lofted the ball and turned.

As always, her stomach dropped when their eyes met. Disheveled and unshaven, he appeared far more dark and dangerous now than the last time she had seen him. But Meg ignored his effect, ignored it in a way she hadn't been able to before. She waved as though her sudden appearance was an everyday occurrence.

He held up his racket as if to defend himself, then, with boyish charm, he opened the door. "What an unexpected surprise, Meg. The two-week deadline doesn't expire for five more days. I am impressed."

"I thought it would work to my advantage if I came to talk to you early," she replied. "Throw you off your game, so to speak. May I come in?"

He raked a hand through his hair, spiking it into tawny, leonine ends. "Certainly there are better places to meet than a squash court. How about upstairs in the club lounge? Give me fifteen minutes and I'll meet you there after I shower and change."

Fifteen minutes for Jack Tarkenton to hatch a defense? No way. "Actually, this is fine," she said, and gestured at the open court.

"Don't be silly, Meg. There's a room nearby that personal trainers use when consulting with their clients. It's got a table and a couple of chairs, and it's very private. I'm sure you'll be more comfortable there."

"But I'm not looking for comfort or privacy, Jack. At least not the kind afforded by a small room. I especially like this Plexiglas." She rapped on the clear surface. "People can see in and I can see out, all while the door is closed. It's the perfect spot for a private tête-à-tête with you."

His grin widened and he held the door open, inviting her in with a flourish. "Come in, then, said the spider to the fly."

She sailed by him. "Thank you."

He closed the door and settled back against it. "I didn't realize you were a member of the club."

"I'm not," she admitted. "I told the woman at the front desk that I was your secretary."

"Lying for us again, Meg? Does that mean you've decided to take me up on my offer?"

"That depends. I have a number of conditions."

"And what might those be?" He wiped his brow with the hem of his shirt, showing off abdominal muscles that were as fit and sculpted as the rest of him.

Meg put her hands behind her back, taking the time to steady herself. He was not going to throw her, not this time. "I concede that you have a right to know your own daughter. I will also concede that it is vitally important to me that Allen retains his rightful place as the father who has raised her. Given the media scrutiny you are subjected to, I understand why a marriage between you and me makes a certain amount of sense. Before I'll consent to your proposal, however, I want two years. The first to properly grieve the death of my husband, and the second to give Katie a chance to know you. Our families will also need to see us together over an extended period of time before they'll accept us as a couple. The second year will provide time for a proper courtship."

"Courtship. What an old-fashioned word."

"Despite the way our relationship began, I happen to be old-fashioned in a number of ways. Since this won't be a match made in heaven, I want the ceremony to be brief. A justice of the peace is fine with me. You should also be made aware that I will not sign a prenuptial agreement that leaves me destitute should the marriage end prematurely. I know my brother signed one when he married your sister, but his financial situation was far more stable than mine. Allen was young enough to think life insurance wasn't necessary. I need to be sure Katie's future is assured.''

''How intelligent of you to plan ahead, Meg.''

''Last but not least, there is one other matter that needs to be discussed. Please listen carefully, Jack, because I will say this only once. We will not be sleeping together. If I discover that you have been less than discreet with any of your affairs, I will file for divorce and take you for every penny I can get. You won't be allowed to taint my life or the life of my child with scandal or your less-than-savory reputation. Is that understood?''

''But, Meg, I've spent thousands of hours in backbreaking labor to establish that reputation. You can't seriously believe I would abandon it so easily.''

''This isn't a joke. I will not allow you to treat me or anything I say as less than important. I have told you I will tolerate some of your habits. Disrespect is not one of them.''

''The matter of my sexual habits is hardly a joking matter. Neither are yours, especially if you are going to be my wife.''

''I think I have made my position clear. If you wish to pretend you don't understand what my reaction will be should you ever darken my bedroom door, that is your problem, not mine.'' Meg tucked her purse under her arm. ''You've been to my house. If you need my phone number, Amanda and Bram have it. You may also find it under the listing for Allen Betz.'' She reached around him to open the door.

His hand closed around her wrist. "Your conditions are not acceptable to me, Meg."

She didn't flinch. "My conditions are not negotiable. You made your proposal, I made mine. It meets the requirements you presented to me. If you want to go back on your word, I can't stop you. But you should know that if you do make that choice, the offer I made today is null and void, and I will opt for a public custody battle."

"If you do, Katie's picture will be plastered on the front page of every newspaper in the country."

"It would be devastating, I agree. Having her exposed as a Tarkenton, particularly an illegitimate Tarkenton, is not something I wish to contemplate. But the truth is preferable to having you dictate how my child and I will live our lives. Though Katie will be enormously confused should joint custody be granted, I will not be blackmailed. And when Katie is old enough, she will know exactly who and what her father is. To paraphrase your words to me, her best interests must always be kept in mind."

She jerked the door open. Jack let her pass and tracked her march across the gym, seeing determination in every stride.

He could stop her, he knew. He could blow her cover and have it out here, in full public view. With the lunch crowd filtering in, there were plenty of witnesses to create a huge scene. Then the tabloids would pick it up and the talk shows and the networks, and in the end, she'd be forced to name him as Katie's father. But that wouldn't give him much satisfaction, nor much pleasure, either. Not where the Widow Betz was concerned.

She'd just drawn a line in the sand. Separate bedrooms, separate lives. If he was going to sacrifice his long-standing bachelorhood, he wasn't sacrificing everything that went along with it. With his daughter came his wife. A wife in every sense of the word.

Meg might need some artful persuasion, but he'd made artful persuasion his career in life. She'd fallen for him once. She would fall for him again.

Katie was one challenge, her mother another. Playing with Meg was getting more and more interesting.

And a helluva lot more fun.

Three

"This is an ambush."

Seized from behind by a very large man, Meg burst out laughing. In front of her, the day-care receptionist's eyes widened, and Meg knew she wasn't the only one to recognize her brother, Bram Masterson, otherwise known professionally as the Beastmaster.

Katie came running across the playroom, where she'd gone to retrieve her coat. "Mommy, Mommy, it's Uncle Bram!"

"How's my favorite girl?" Bram asked, picking Katie up in mid-flight and tossing her above his head.

Katie giggled in answer. Catching her, Bram set her in the crook of his thickly muscled arm. Meg marveled at his easy strength. All three of her brothers were good-size men, but Bram had the bigness and brawn of a professional athlete. Which he was.

His opponents might have monikers like the Bulkster and Six Billion Dollar Man, but what he did inside a pro wrestling ring made him one of the biggest stars of pay-per-view television.

"It's the Beastmaster!" a little boy cried.

Swarmed by a dozen preschoolers, Bram got down on his knees, wrestling with them, pretending to let them take him down. His gentleness was as great as his size, and seeing Katie jump on top of him made Meg smile in genuine delight, something she hadn't done in weeks.

"I see Katie's been captured. How about you?"

At the sound of Jack's voice, Meg's smile abruptly died, while the poor receptionist went absolutely boggle-eyed. The Beastmaster was small potatoes compared to the unique and elite celebrity who represented the American version of royalty, the Tarkentons.

"Why, hello, Jack," Meg said evenly. "This is a surprise."

"A pleasant one, I trust."

Unlike her brother, Jack was dressed one step above casual, one step into serious chic. The sienna shirt had no collar and probably no label, either, it fit so well. His sand beige linen jacket also looked custom-made. As an expert in the art of textiles, she certainly recognized the fabric. Woven in Damascus by hand, it was among the costliest in the world. She raised an eyebrow. "How long has it been since we last saw each other? Surely no more than a couple of days."

"Meg, being apart from you for one day is like a year for me. I couldn't wait to see you again."

Meg wagged her finger at him, all too aware of

the boggle-eyed receptionist. "Now, Jack. I wouldn't want anyone to get the wrong idea about us. Especially my big brother."

"That's why I brought him along. We're going to kidnap you."

"Really? Is that the plan?" Meg looked to Bram as he extricated himself from the pack of preschoolers.

"I told you this was an ambush," Bram said, helping Katie put on her coat. "Amanda is in town, and J.J. and I drove down from Bedford to meet her. We'll be staying at Jack's apartment for a couple of days and hoped you'd join us for dinner. Katie, do you remember J.J.'s uncle Jack? He's your Aunt Amanda's little brother."

Katie looked up at Jack with solemn eyes. "You're not little."

"But I can be." Jack crouched and completed the introductions by matching Katie's solemnity and formally offering to shake her hand. Katie gave it after the slightest hesitation.

Meg searched her brother's face. Was he somehow in cahoots with Jack? "Why isn't Amanda in D.C.? I thought Congress was in session this week."

"Now that she's on the Foreign Relations Committee, she has to come to New York periodically for meetings at the UN. She ended up staying late last night and doesn't have to be back at the Capitol until Monday. I won't be on the road until next weekend, so J.J. and I drove up to see her."

"How about it, Katie?" Jack asked. "Would you like to come over to my apartment and see J.J.?"

"Can I, Mommy?"

That clinched it for Meg. Not only was he making

mincemeat of the conditions she'd set, he was using Katie to do it. "I'm sorry, sweetheart, but we need to go straight home tonight. Maybe some other time."

Bram held the door open for them. "Amanda and I get so few opportunities to see the two of you, Meg. What's the rush?"

"There's no rush. I'm just tired, that's all. It's been a long day."

"You don't want to make it longer by riding a commuter bus back to Jersey with Katie on your lap," countered Bram. "Jack keeps a car here in town. I'll drive you home after the traffic dies down."

"Or you and Katie are welcome to spend the night at my place," Jack offered. "I'll drive you home tomorrow myself. How's that for service?"

"Spending the night is definitely out," Meg retorted flatly.

Bram put a companionable arm around her shoulders. "Come on, honey. Have dinner with us. Put your feet up for a while, say hello to Amanda and J.J., and give yourself a little R and R."

"Please, Mommy?" Katie asked, tugging Meg's hand. "I want to play with J.J."

Meg glanced pointedly at Jack. "We can't stay very long. I want to make that clear."

Jack raised his hands in surrender. "Whatever you say, Meg."

Whatever you say, my eye. Meg faced her brother. "Katie and I will need to leave right after dinner."

"No problem," replied Bram. "I'll have you home in record time."

It turned out Jack lived in Midtown, only a few

blocks away. Judging by the historic stonework on his apartment building, it dated back to the turn of the century and had been restored to its original grandeur. A doorman jumped to usher "Mr. Tarkenton and his guests" inside. The security guard monitoring the lobby treated him with unusual familiarity, greeting both Jack and Bram by name.

The old-fashioned cage of an elevator was manned by a uniformed operator. She asked if Katie wanted to help pull the lever that closed the fancy ironwork doors. Of course, Katie did, and when Jack pointed at the floor numbers above the elevator doors, she counted up with him in unison.

Studying his profile, Meg tried to assess his motives. She hadn't expected him to barge into her life again this soon. Clearly he was trying to get to Katie. Clearly he wasn't above using Bram, Amanda and J.J. to do it. But why now?

The elevator doors clanged open, revealing a living room so large, the main floor of her house could have fit inside it. His so-called apartment took up the entire penthouse floor.

"Katie!"

Three-year-old J.J. catapulted from his seat on the thick dove gray carpet. Amanda rescued the playing cards that scattered in his wake and rose herself, barefoot in blue jeans and a fuzzy mohair sweater that gave her a girlish air despite the classic French twist of her blond hair. "Meg," she said, extending her hands. "I'm so glad you and Katie could make it."

Smiling, Meg caught those hands, and they kissed each other cheek to cheek, as the French did, engendering a nostalgic pang for the culture of her beloved France.

Amanda scooped Katie up. "My goodness, Miss Katie. When did you start getting so grown-up?"

J.J. excitedly jumped up and down, tugging on Katie's dress. "Katie, Katie, Katie," he chanted.

"Hey, sport, how about we give our special guests a chance to come inside." Jack zoomed J.J. across the room as if he were an airplane.

It didn't appear to be put on for her benefit, but Meg still suspected Jack's motives. If nothing else, this visit would allow her to see how he handled the children.

His decorative tastes ran toward the traditional, for the apartment was furnished in the same style as his Wall Street office. Mahogany and cherry wood predominated, with upholstered pieces in cream or gold brocade. Glazed lemon yellow, the walls were trimmed by white molding that framed tall windows filmy with sheer drapes.

Amanda led the way to a pair of overstuffed sofas and invited Meg to sit down. The butler's table between them was covered by a thick towel, heaped high with toy cars and trucks. "Nice child-proofing," Meg noted.

"Isn't it, though? Fortunately, Jack doesn't mind. J.J., would you like to show Katie your cars?"

J.J. came running. "My cars!"

Bram slowed him, saving a collision with the table, and gathered up the ends of the towel, sacking the toys. "I think the children and I will retire to the entertainment room," he said, exchanging amused looks with his wife. "If I'm not mistaken, a certain purple dinosaur is making an appearance on our favorite television channel.''

Amanda clasped her hands and put them over her heart. "You have earned my eternal gratitude, dear husband. Let me know when reinforcements are required."

Seeing their obvious love and affection for each other brought a lump to Meg's throat. She had never met a woman more secure with who she was and what she wanted than Amanda. Her brother was just as headstrong. Yet they served as perfect foils for each other, sharing a partnership so strong, Meg had to look away.

Her gaze touched on Jack, with his inscrutable expression and idle stance. If she did marry him, it would be at the cost of such happiness. At least when she married Allen, she had been operating under the youthful delusion that given time, she would come to love her husband. She knew better now.

"Meg, would you like a drink?" Jack asked.

Startled by the hand he placed on her shoulder, she said the first thing that came to mind. "Scotch and soda, please."

"Amanda?" he asked.

"Refresh mine, will you, Jack?" She held out her glass.

"Certainly." He retrieved the glass, letting the lingering warmth of his other hand brand Meg's back. The clink of ice against glass and the swift pouring of liquid heralded his return, as did the rise of fine hairs at the base of her neck.

He delivered her drink first, leaning over her shoulder. Meg cradled the glass with both hands, trying to appear perfectly at ease in front of Amanda.

More clinking, then he ambled into view carrying two glasses. Handing one to Amanda, he set himself on the arm of the couch. "How's the Scotch and soda, Meg?"

"Fine," she replied, sipping her drink. Icy cold, it was far too strong. She thumped the drink onto the coffee table, resolved not to pick it up again. The man was baiting her with his sister not three feet away. "What are you drinking, Jack?" Meg asked.

"Mineral water."

"Really? I didn't realize you don't drink."

"I do, on occasion." He toasted her with his glass and stretched his arm along the back of the couch. "Despite the many reports to the contrary."

Amanda chuckled. "Meg, let me tell you the real reason why my brother doesn't like to drink alcohol. It's all because of our mother."

Meg arched an eyebrow at him. "Your mother?"

"You know what an upstanding citizen of the world she is," Amanda continued. "I've seen her angry only a few occasions in my life. The last time was when one of those supermarket tabloids reported Jack was in the Betty Ford Clinic for the tenth time in two years, dealing with his alcohol problem."

"You have an alcohol problem?" Meg asked Jack directly.

"Some reporters like to think so," he replied. "Normally my mother shrugs off that type of garbage, but she drew the line on the alcohol story. She picked up the phone and called the head of the conglomerate that published this particular newspaper."

"Now, Jack," Amanda chided. "Remember what mother said. You mustn't call it a newspaper."

"Mother called the CEO of this particular *tabloid*

and told him if she ever saw such rubbish about a member of her family printed by him again, she would sue not only his publishing company but him personally. She then pointed out the fact that she was one of the few people in the country wealthy enough to do so.''

"Did it go that far?'' Meg asked.

"Oh, no,'' answered Amanda. "Mother was only bluffing. She's well off, but certainly not wealthy enough to take down a billion dollar conglomerate. She gives that impression, however, with that iron-clad dignity of hers. Of course, Jack had to back her at her word. Since he's constantly dogged by dozens of photographers, he can't be caught drinking *anything*.''

Meg eyed his glass. "Not even mineral water?''

"They say it's spiked with vodka or rum,'' Jack said. "Same with soft drinks, even if I'm drinking from an aluminum can. Such is the power of the press. A picture is worth a thousand lies, and I certainly don't want to make my mother out to be a liar, now, do I?''

"So you really are noble at heart,'' Meg concluded dryly.

Amanda gave him a sisterly poke. "I'm not so sure about that. You should see the young women he's escorted around town. Jack, really. You're much too old for teenagers.''

"What do you say, Meg?'' Jack asked. "Do I need to be more discriminating? Is it time to vacate my title of 'the most eligible bachelor on earth'?''

Amanda snorted. "Meg, don't answer. He proclaimed long ago that there wasn't a woman alive good enough to marry him. Mother concurs. Jack is her only begotten son, after all. She has let it be known, however, that she is willing to overlook a few minor shortcomings in exchange for several more grandchildren. The Tarkenton name must be carried on.''

''The Tarkenton legend must be carried on as well,'' Jack said, draining his glass. ''Something you, my dear sister, handle with your usual aplomb. Well, ladies, I hate to leave your company, but duty calls. I need to check with my staff about dinner.''

''Staff?'' Meg inquired when he was out of earshot.

''It's not nearly as grand as it sounds. He has a part-time cook and full-time maid. The latter lives in, since he's gone so much.''

''Does he travel a lot?''

''Constantly. Monaco's a favorite. So are Rio, Bangkok, Hong Kong. He doesn't stay anywhere long. He wants people to think all he cares about are fast cars and fast women.''

''That's not true?''

''See? Even you think he's beyond hope, and you're one of the most perceptive people I know.''

''Amanda, you're a United States senator, for heaven's sake. You size people up in an instant.''

''Yes, but I don't see with the depth you do. You know the difference between the purely ornamental and the truly authentic, and that is a rare quality in this world.''

''Because of my education in art?''

''That's part of it. Certainly, your studies abroad refined your ability to see things as they really are. But it's more than that. Nothing has been handed to you on a silver platter, yet you have spent your life immersed in the richness of our culture. And you did it on your own, at a relatively young age.''

''When I left home to take that scholarship at the Sorbonne, I might not have been close to my family geographically, but I was in spirit. I certainly never felt like I was completely on my own.''

''That's what makes you unique, Meg. Your family encouraged and supported you every step of the way, even though there was no guarantee of success. Do you know how extraordinary that is?''

''I owe my family, particularly my mother, everything. But isn't that what families are for? You and Bram, for example. You both have demanding careers, yet manage to make time to be together at a moment's notice, like today. To know that such love exists…'' Meg broke off, overwhelmed by her yearning for what she had never had.

Amanda took her hand. ''It's Allen, isn't it? You must miss him terribly.''

Meg couldn't deny it. Not when she had to pretend that she had loved her late husband with all her heart. But her real sorrow was about the depth of emotion she and Allen had never had, had never experienced, had never shared. That same lack of depth would exist in her marriage to Jack. She couldn't confess the truth to Amanda, though. So many secrets. So many lies.

''Meg, you were the best thing that ever happened to Allen,'' Amanda said softly. ''You and Katie both. Don't ever forget that.''

Rather than spill her heart, Meg murmured something about checking on Katie and left the room. But once she gained the hall, Meg sought someplace where she could be alone and out of sight. She entered the nearest room, but didn't switch on the light. She just huddled inside.

What was she going to do? The events of the evening proved that Jack wasn't going to change his ways. And she didn't think she had the strength to survive another loveless marriage, even if it was in Katie's best interest. The first time around, she'd been pregnant and foolish enough to believe that she could learn to love Allen. The road to hell really was paved with good intentions. During her marriage, she had never felt more lonely in her life.

"Why, Meg, I've been looking all over for you." Turning on the light and joining her in the bathroom, Jack closed the door behind him.

Unable to believe his timing, much less the place he chose to exercise it, Meg put her hands on her hips. "What do you think you are doing?"

"Courtship, remember?" he said, advancing on her.

Meg raised her hands, keeping him at arm's length. "This isn't courtship, it's coercion, and it's much too soon."

"Too soon?" He took her hands and, kissing the back of them, crowded her into the corner. "You accepted my proposal. We are getting married, aren't we?"

"In two years, Jack," she hissed, pushing at him. "I made it perfectly clear when I last saw you—"

"Two years is much too long, Meg," he said, leaning in and invading what little remained of her space. "I won't even wait one year. Six months is stretching it. I'd rather be married in six weeks."

"Six weeks!" she gasped. "Are you out of your mind?"

"As a matter of fact, I am. Over you." He forced her hands down and nuzzled her neck. "Doesn't that tell you something, Meg? Doesn't it give you a thrill?"

"What you're telling me is that you have no respect for me and my feelings. We are not officially engaged and won't be, either, if you keep acting this way. Now, back off."

He didn't. He pressed closer, trapping her against the wall with his weight. If she screamed, Bram would come running, but what would it solve? She needed more time, more space, a clearer head. She couldn't have any of that with Jack cornering her like this.

"Look, I'm not going to do this with you," she said, straining to keep her voice low and under control. "We need a more appropriate time and place to have this discussion. Let's do lunch. I'm willing to compromise if you are."

"This place seems perfectly appropriate to me."

"Jack, please," she appealed directly, meeting the dark pools of his intense eyes. "Don't do this."

"Don't do what, Meg?"

"This," she choked, turning her face to avoid his. But the whisper of his breath stirred her hair, stirred her heart. It had been so long.

"This?" he echoed, his mouth warm on the shell of her ear. "Or this?" Trailing tender kisses along the line of her cheek, he stroked her neck where her pulse revealed her swiftly beating heart.

She closed her eyes, unwilling to bear the feeling, for she hurt inside, hurt for all the times she'd fantasized about being caressed by this man when Allen had touched her, groped her. She had tried to love her husband. But she had to trick her body with fantasies of another to do it.

Jack. It had always been Jack.

"Meg, you're trembling." He laid his hand on the side of her face and nuzzled her there. "I won't hurt you. You know that, don't you?"

But it wasn't bodily harm he threatened her with. It was the smoke of his voice, the feel and scent of him filling her lungs, hammering her heart, heating her skin.

He knew it, too. He whispered how beautiful she was, how luminous, like a great work of art, fine and rare. Kissing her, he traced the bone of her jaw, the shape of her nose, the outline of her lips.

It felt so good.

Meg shut her eyes to concentrate, to keep hold of who she was and what she wanted, and she didn't want this, not this way, not with him. It wasn't right that Jack pushed her like this, that he took what she wasn't ready to give.

Still, she didn't move. He stroked and kissed and did what he wanted, and the knowledge made Meg tremble inside, tremble because she didn't want him to stop.

It was humiliating to stand there with her face turned aside and her back against the wall and feel the yearning of full-fledged desire. Her body thrummed with it. The hand she managed to wedge between them clutched at his shirt, clutched at the strength of the silk, clutched at his heat mixing with her own.

She had to hold on, had to fight back, had to ignore the power of his words and his mouth and his body and his mind. She had to remember Katie.

"No!" she shouted, and shoved, ducking by him. But he was behind her in seconds, snagging her waist and bringing her back, cradling her against the hard arousal of his body.

"Let's marry next week, Meg," he whispered in her ear. "Neither one of us can wait any longer."

With a cry, she elbowed him and wrenched out the door, down the hall, into the wall that was her brother. Bram caught her in mid-flight. "Meg? What is it?"

She covered her mouth and choked back all sound, but the grimness in Bram's face told the story as he looked beyond her.

"What the hell is going on here?" he demanded.

"What does it look like?" came Jack's cool reply.

Meg grasped at her brother's clenched fists. "Bram, it's okay. I'm all right."

"No, you're not." He looked down at her, the green in his eyes sparking in concern. "Tell me what happened."

"Nothing. Nothing happened. Where's Katie? We have to get home."

She felt Bram's anger in his tightening grip. "Did he make a move on you? Is that what this is about?"

"Bram, please," Meg begged. "Just come with me."

He didn't budge but looked past her, pointing his finger at Jack. "You stay away from my sister, you hear?"

"Your sister doesn't want me to stay away from her."

"I don't care what your excuse is—stay away from her or you'll answer to me. Come on, Meg."

He towed her unceremoniously down the hall, calling for Katie. Amanda appeared as they entered the living room, but her smile vanished the moment she saw them. "Bram, what's wrong?"

"It's your damned brother. Where the hell are his car keys?"

"Here," Jack answered, entering the living room hand in hand with Katie. "Uncle Bram is going to take you and your mom home now, Katie. Will you give him these keys, please?"

"Okay." Katie skipped across the room, jingling the keys happily, while the two men stared at each other.

"Watch yourself, Jack," Bram warned. "I don't want you anywhere near them."

"That might be a little tough, since Meg and I have recently started seeing each other," Jack replied evenly. "In fact, my mother has agreed to invite her and Katie to join us for Thanksgiving dinner. Bram, I'm sure you'll approve. Meg and Katie are, after all, *family*."

Four

"Let's not have this conversation in front of Katie, Bram," Meg said as they settled into Jack's sleek black Jaguar.

Bram gunned the engine and backed out of the underground parking space, tires squealing. Katie piped up from where she was strapped in the back seat. "Mommy, are you and Uncle Bram having a fight?"

"No, sweetheart. We're just talking."

Bram swung the car up the exit ramp. "Meg, you may as well tell her the truth, because I'm not leaving this alone."

"You'd better leave it alone," Meg retorted. She refused to allow him to malign Jack within Katie's hearing. "You may be my big brother, but you're not my keeper."

"He's no good for you, Meg. You've got to know that."

"So noted. You've done your good deed for the day. Now, if you mention his name again, I'll march right back to that penthouse apartment and have him drive me home instead of you."

"What are you thinking? The man is the exact opposite of Allen. The life-style, the jet-setting, the women—"

"Bram," Meg warned. "That's enough."

"I can't believe you're defending him. I can't believe you've been seeing him. When did this start?"

"None of your business."

"None of my business? Since when did you get so stubborn?"

"Mommy, what's stubborn?" Katie asked.

Meg cast a sidelong glance at Bram. "It means you are not *listening* very well."

Bram moved through the late-night traffic to the Lincoln Tunnel with aggressive ease. "I want what's best for you, Meg," he grated. "You and Katie."

"You think I don't?" She flipped on the radio, but the tension between them remained thick enough to cut with a knife. Meg couldn't blame him, either. She'd barreled out of the bathroom as though she was being chased by the devil, which she was.

How could she have let Jack kiss her like that? And the things he'd said. He was crazy to think she'd marry him any time in the near future. Yet her heart was beating and her palms were sweaty, and worse, the powerful vibration of the car's engine made her body's response all the more scandalous.

She refused to look at Bram, much less Katie, not when she was red-faced with mortification. Clearly, she couldn't control Jack. She could barely control herself.

Thanksgiving was less than three weeks away. Was it possible to make herself immune to him by then? Their affair had been intense, but she didn't remember this tumult of heat and blood singing through her veins. All he had to do was touch her and she started panting like one of Pavlov's dogs. Lust to the nth degree.

Except lust meant absolutely nothing. He was the one who'd taught her that great lesson, lo, those many years ago. She was merely another conquest, a pawn he used in the games he played.

Meg crossed her arms. So she got a little hot. So he noticed. Big deal. It wasn't a crime. Lots of women found him attractive. He wasn't called the most eligible bachelor on earth for nothing.

So what if she was physically attracted to him? Okay, that might be a slight understatement, but the point was, she wasn't in love with the guy. She was in lust. Plain old manageable lust. A workout here, a cold shower there. Her heart was not involved. Not her inner heart, where Katie and the other people she loved lived.

Jack Tarkenton wasn't one of those people. And he wasn't going to be, either, not if he pulled another stunt like he did tonight.

The passing lights of the city came into better focus and Meg breathed deeply, striving for control. Her number one concern was Katie. What was best for her?

Tilted in the back seat, she lay asleep, her head resting against the door, sooty-colored lashes spread on apple red cheeks. Jack hadn't been anywhere nearly as aggressive with her. He wasn't showering her with gifts, wasn't overwhelming her with attention. If he truly was sincere about having Katie's best interests at heart, then Meg had to admit the ambush he engineered was made far less traumatic by the inclusion of Bram, Amanda and J.J.

Most important, Jack was honoring his promise not to force the issue of paternity. As long as he kept his word on that score, Meg was bound and determined to keep hers.

He had caught her off guard tonight. Next time she saw him, she had to be ready for anything. She had to make him play by her rules, not his. Next time they were together, she was going to be prepared.

To Meg, prepared meant wearing loose-fitting winter white slacks, a matching tunic sweater and chaste pearl button earrings.

Prepared also meant contributing to the Thanksgiving meal. She didn't want to feel the least bit beholden to any of the Tarkentons. Snuggled in the hatchback of her Honda Civic was a high-crusted homemade pie filled with cinnamon-scented apples. Katie was so proud of having helped make it, she wanted to present it to the Tarkentons herself.

One look at the enormity of their Southampton estate, however, and Meg wondered if that was such a good idea. Sitting like a castle upon a hill, the Roman-inspired, white-columned mansion was surrounded by acres and acres of rolling grounds. Thick stands of evergreens and winter-naked elms intermittently cut off her view, as did the heavy posts of the intricately carved ironwork fence, but that didn't stop Meg's rising sense of awe...and nervousness.

Bram had never mentioned wealth or security like this.

The closer she got to the entrance gate, the more she slowed the car. Straddling the middle of the gate was a slant-roofed guardhouse, manned by an actual guard. His stiff-visored hat dipped as he took note of her license plate number.

Katie sat up and looked around, rubbing her eyes. "Are we there yet, Mommy?"

"I think so, sweetie," Meg responded with forced cheerfulness. She would look like a coward if she turned around now. Easing the car up to the gate, she lowered her window to speak to the guard and inhaled sharply at the blast of frigid air. No Thanksgiving for this poor man.

"Name, please?" he asked.

"I'm Meg Betz and this is my daughter, Katie."

His breath fogged in the chill as he checked the information against his clipboard. "Meg Masterson Betz?"

"That's my full name, yes."

He touched the brim of his hat and opened the gate.

Negotiating the serpentine road to the top of the hill took a full five minutes. The road emptied to a circular drive in front of the mansion, and Meg bit her lip when she saw the layout. Fifty feet of flagstones lay between the driveway and the colonnaded entrance. Icy, uneven flagstones. To let Katie carry the pie up that long walk courted disaster.

The valet who met the car appeared to agree. He opened the passenger door and helped Katie out. "Watch your step, little honey. It's slick out today."

Rather than wait for the valet to come round to

open her door, Meg scooped up the foil-wrapped pie and exited. If she was lucky, Katie would be too caught up in the majesty of their surroundings to remember the pie.

Thanking the valet, Meg took Katie's hand.

"Mommy, I want to carry the pie."

"It's a long way to the front door, sweetheart. Tell you what. I'll carry the pie to the house, then you can have your turn and bring it inside."

Katie halted in her tracks. "But you said I could carry it by myself!"

"I didn't know we'd have to walk so far, sweetie."

"But you promised!" Fat tears welled in her eyes.

Meg considered giving in. The last thing either of them needed was a tantrum at the Tarkenton's front door. And it was Thanksgiving, after all. But if Katie dropped the pie or, worse, fell, she'd be inconsolable. She had utterly rejected wearing her winter boots, too, refusing to get into the car when Meg had suggested bringing them "just in case."

Those patent leather shoes of hers might be pretty, but they were not in the least practical. And Katie wanted to wear them all the time. The price of vanity would be brought home far more effectively by this situation than continuous battles whenever they ventured outside.

"I'm sorry, Katie, but no. It's very cold and icy out. Since I'm the only one wearing boots, I will carry the pie."

The tantrum was in full swing by the time they made it safely to the mansion's front door. Meg left the stupid pie on a wrought-iron bench on the porch and picked Katie up, hoping to distract her with the prospect of lifting the big brass knocker centering the middle of the massive front door.

The plan was foiled when the door opened of its own accord.

With a guard at the gate and a valet for the car, Meg expected a housekeeper. Instead, the matriarch of the Tarkenton family welcomed them in all her graceful splendor.

"Come in, come in," Eleanor Tarkenton said, her famous blue eyes crinkling with her patrician smile. Silver-blond hair was piled on her head like a coronet. She wore a long cardigan of butter-colored wool over a soft brown pantsuit, accented by necklaces of gold.

Meg stepped inside, embarrassed to the bone, holding the wailing Katie. So much for making a good first impression.

"I'm sorry about my daughter. She'll be fine in a minute. We brought a pie. It's on the bench outside—"

Jack's deep voice cut through the din. "Allow me…"

The sleek ebony of his cashmere turtleneck and tight charcoal jeans should have overwhelmed someone with his blond coloring. Unfortunately, Jack Tarkenton wasn't just someone. He retrieved the pie, handed it to his mother and shut the door in one fell swoop, then whisked Katie into his arms.

She halted in mid-scream and blinked at him with wide, wet eyes. "Hi, Katie," he said. "Remember me? I'm J.J.'s Uncle Jack. This is my mother, Eleanor. She likes to be called Grandma, but she'll answer to Oscar the Grouch, too."

Meg held her breath. Katie, however, did not. Her

next scream was the loudest one yet. Frowning, Jack had no choice but to relinquish her, and Meg took her back, allowing Katie to resort to her old habit of sucking her thumb in order to quiet her. But the damage was already done, and in the awkwardness of the moment, Meg tried to explain. "Katie's pretty shy with strangers."

Jack flinched at the remark, making Meg realize how her feeble excuse struck home in a way she never intended. Fortunately, his mother retrieved the situation with gracious good humor. "It appears my son is not quite the lady-killer he seems to think," said Eleanor.

"Apparently not," he agreed. "Mother, you remember Bram's sister, the ever-lovely Meg Masterson."

Put on guard by this salvo, Meg offered her hand. "Meg Masterson Betz," she amended with a smile. "Thank you for including Katie and me in your family celebration, Mrs. Tarkenton."

"Please call me Eleanor, my dear," she said. "You and your daughter are already part of our family with your brother here, along with Amanda and, of course, little J.J. We're happy to have you share the day with us."

She ushered them further into the magnificent palazzo-style foyer. The Italian influence extended into a huge formal living room, decorated in Florentine tones of gilt and olive green. Laid out in the dining room beyond, Baccarat and gold plate glittered in holiday profusion.

A maid appeared from nowhere to take their coats. Overwhelmed by the grandeur of it all, Meg set Katie on the ground. Jack crouched next to her and pointed out the chandelier suspended above.

It was easy for Meg to see why. Hundreds of crystals threw rainbows on the high domed ceiling, creating a light all their own. Entranced, Katie tipped her head back.

Meg's heart skipped a beat. The resemblance between father and daughter was subtle, but it was there. The color of their eyes, the way they turned their heads. Meg glanced at Eleanor. What, if anything, had Jack told her?

"You have a beautiful home, Eleanor," Meg said.

"Thank you, my dear," Eleanor replied, showing them into a long hall off the foyer. "My husband and I bought this house soon after Amanda was born. John so loved the country. The memories I have of him here have steadied me in the years since his death. I was so sorry to hear of your own husband's passing."

Meg pressed her hand, moved by her obvious sincerity. "Thank you."

She linked arms with Meg. "I know the holidays can be a difficult time. Please consider joining us for Christmas Eve. It is a tradition in our family to open gifts then."

"Except the ones that Santa Claus brings," Jack added, coming abreast with Katie at his side.

Wondering if he had provided the impetus behind the invitation, Meg decided to nip this presumptuous attitude of his in the bud. "I'm afraid Katie and I have other plans."

Katie tugged Jack's sleeve. "Where's J.J.? Mommy says she'll take us to see Santa Claus. I want to tell him."

"Coming right up." Taking her hand, Jack led Katie down the hall, calling for J.J.

"What a beautiful child," Eleanor commented.

"Thank you," Meg said, struck by the bittersweet realization that there was a subtle resemblance between Eleanor and Katie as well. "I apologize for her behavior when we arrived. She and I were involved in a bit of a contretemps on our way in."

"With the raising of my own children, I know how these things happen." She patted Meg's hand, smiling with the aspect of shared experience. "I understand you and my son have struck up quite a relationship."

"It's more an acquaintance than anything else," Meg hedged, looking ahead. Of course, Jack was nowhere to be seen, having disappeared with Katie through an archway at the end of the hall.

"I hope I don't presume too much by giving you my blessing," Eleanor continued. "You have my prayers as well."

Meg tried to appear nonchalant. "I'm not sure if I should be alarmed by that or not."

"Not alarmed, my dear. Careful. He takes after his father in many ways. Perhaps too many. But you will be good for him, I think, you and your daughter. Please reconsider coming here for Christmas Eve. We really would love to have you."

Meg hesitated. "To tell you the truth, this is Katie's first Christmas without her father. I'm not sure how she'll react under the circumstances. Please understand."

"We understand perfectly, don't we, Mother?"

A heavy arm descended across Meg's shoulders as Jack gave her an overly affectionate squeeze. She wanted to sink into the floor. Ten minutes in and she'd managed to put her foot in her mouth twice while he was up to his same old tricks. She couldn't plead her case, either, not with his mother there.

He steered them both into a room Meg could only describe as an informal library. Lined with shelves upon shelves of leather-bound books, the room was dominated by a fireplace on one side, while a theater-size TV dominated the other. Comfortably large burgundy leather sofas and chairs were scattered around, and in one cleared corner, Katie was already hard at work with J.J., building a tower from a huge pile of wooden blocks.

Bram left his seat in front of the televised football game and greeted Meg warmly with one of his patented bear hugs. He eyed her more critically than usual, however, and Meg knew she was in for a very long day when Bram turned the same critical eye on Jack.

Thankfully, Amanda shooed the men toward the football game. "Meg, you look smashing, as always," she said, following her mother's lead to a cozy grouping of wing chairs in front of the fireplace. "As usual, I'm dying to know where you got that outfit."

"Trade secret," Meg said with a wink.

"Mother, would you believe that this woman gets to choose from the latest in designer fashions? Meg, tell her what you do for a living."

"When the fashion houses start planning their collections, I work with textile manufacturers to produce the fabrics and colors the designers are looking for. It does allow me to see what will be paraded down the runways during the next season, but I'm afraid a sample from one of my sources is the closest I've come to a designer original.''

''Meg, you're being far too modest,'' Amanda scolded. ''Mother, you may remember that when Bram and I married, Meg had just graduated from the Sorbonne. She's an expert in historical textiles and works to preserve the traditional ways of making the fine fabrics of old. She is a true *artiste*.''

''As are you, Amanda, when it comes to politics,'' Meg replied, smiling. ''How go the wars in D.C.?''

They chatted amiably, giving Meg a chance to measure the ongoing tension between Bram and Jack. Unfortunately, their competitive natures weren't likely to take an ultimatum from her with grace. And Jack would jump on any weakness on her part, just like he did the last time they were together. She wasn't about to let that happen again. But she couldn't ignore their animosity, either. By the end of the day, she'd be an absolute wreck.

When Jack headed for the refreshment table, Meg checked to ensure Katie was fully engrossed in playing with J.J. and excused herself, making a beeline toward Jack. Bram made a move to intercept her, rising from the couch, but Meg shook her head at him and he stayed where he was—though he watched her like the proverbial hawk.

Jack watched her, too, though he was much more casual about it, sipping from a bottle of mineral water as she approached. Judging by the early and obvious way Meg was singling him out, Jack guessed what she had on her mind. But he'd be damned before he let her zing him again. ''Hello, Meg,'' he said cordially. ''I feel I should echo the sentiments of my mother and sister. Glad you and Katie could make it.''

''Thank you for the kind invitation,'' she replied smoothly.

''You are welcome.''

''Am I really?''

The mischievous blue of her eyes took the bite off the query, but Jack knew feminine directness when he heard it. ''Rest assured, Meg,'' he answered, saluting her by raising his bottle of water, ''you and Katie will always be welcome here.''

''After what happened the last time you and I were alone together, I wasn't certain that would be the case.''

Censure delivered with such genteel decorum deserved wryness of the highest order. ''Consider me properly chastised, then.''

''I find an apology is in order as well.''

''For my numerous transgressions, no doubt.''

She pounced on that with a delicately arched brow. ''Actually...I was the one who transgressed.''

Her air of genuine contrition put him on instant alert. The last thing he wanted was a mea culpa from Meg. ''An apology isn't necessary, especially from you,'' he said flatly. ''I have enough to make up for as it is.''

''All the same, I do want to apologize. I didn't mean to offend you when I made that remark implying you and Katie were complete strangers.''

''We are strangers,'' he returned bluntly. ''Thanks to you.''

That stopped her, if only for a moment. ''Look, Jack,'' she said softly, ''I didn't come here to fight with you. I made a mistake and I'm sorry. It was not in the least—''

"Save the apologies for our honeymoon, Meg. You might have something to bargain with then.''

Like his mother, who had the moral authority to carry off a show of great offense, Meg frosted him with one look. Turning her back, she walked away without another word. It wasn't a retreat, he realized, but a choice. And it made him ashamed of his.

Meg took refuge on the couch beside Bram, but her growing sense of despair didn't lift, even when they were called for Thanksgiving dinner. Jack played the role of the good host to the hilt, insisting she and Katie sit next to each other at the table. If he meant to make amends, it came far too late for Meg.

Declaring himself J.J.'s official dinner partner, Jack kept him busy throughout the interminable serving of the many courses. His patience should have warmed her; it shook her instead. Jack didn't deserve to be Katie's father. Unfortunately, that didn't change the fact that he was.

Dessert finally came and the pies were brought out. Katie proudly pointed to their contribution. "It's apple," she proclaimed. "I made it all by myself.''

"Katie, will you cut me a piece, please?" Jack asked. "Apple pie's my favorite.''

"Mine, too!" J.J. added.

Meg supervised the cutting. Katie managed the wedges all right but needed help to lever them out and transfer them safely onto china plates. Carrying each one with both hands, she served all those who requested apple pie. When the time came to eat her own piece, she carried her plate to J.J. and Jack.

"I want to eat with you guys," she declared.

Jack lifted her onto his knee. The sight of the two of them together was too much. To Meg, the chatter and clatter of dinner faded away as his knack with children became more apparent.

Escaping from the table, Meg started crying long before she made it to the powder room. Fortunately, there was no one to see her tears. The entire household was involved with the Thanksgiving meal.

She locked the door behind her, but there was no place to hide, not from the truth. She couldn't keep Katie from her own father. Not when he demonstrated how capable he was of fulfilling the role.

Meg splashed water on her face, but the collar of her tunic tightened like a noose around her neck. Marrying Jack was out of the question now. He baited her every chance he got, playing stupid games of one-upmanship. But he wasn't going to give up Katie without a fight. She'd be caught in the middle of a major and very public custody battle, her life forever altered by the ugliness of scandal.

The scandal wouldn't end there, either, Meg realized. Every member of the Tarkenton and Masterson families would be forced to take sides, especially Bram, Amanda and J.J.

Her blood. Her family. And what of Katie's blood, Katie's family?

A brisk knock sounded on the door. "Meg?"

There was no mistaking the emphatic sound of Jack's voice. Meg flung open the door, ready to give him a piece of her mind, only to find him crouched on the floor next to a very distraught Katie. She launched herself into Meg's arms.

"Mommy, Mommy, I thought you left! I thought you left!"

Meg dropped to her knees, hugging Katie close. "Oh, baby, Mommy would never leave you. Never, ever." Even with Jack there as witness, Meg couldn't contain her flood of tears. Katie sensed them, too, and pulled back in alarm.

"Mommy, why are you crying?"

"I'm just sad, honey. You know how people cry when they are sad."

Katie's lips quivered and she cried, too, and Meg held her tight, guilty and angry at the man who had caused this misery in the first place. Jack actually had the gall to push his handkerchief on her.

Meg rose with Katie in her arms, refusing to so much as acknowledge him. "Let's go say goodbye to everybody, sweetie, shall we?"

"Meg, wait." He dared put a hand on her arm. "I want to show you something. You, too, Katie," he added. "A surprise."

Meg didn't have any trouble facing him squarely then. "No," she replied, glaring. "We're leaving."

"What kind of surprise?" Katie wanted to know.

"Something beautiful," he said, though his gaze remained on Meg. "Beautiful like you and your mommy."

Meg clutched Katie like the lifeline she was. "When I said no, I meant no. You are not doing this to me again, Jack," she said through her teeth.

"But, Mommy, it's beautiful." Katie's little hand patted Meg's cheek. "Beautiful like us."

"I'm asking, Meg," Jack said. "For Katie's sake."

"Please, Mommy? It will make you happy again."

Meg felt the depth of her daughter's plea and locked gazes with Jack. "This changes nothing," she said. "Do you understand?"

He nodded and gave her a wide berth, leading the way up the winding staircase to the second floor. Katie showed excitement, straining to follow. But then Katie had a child's trusting heart. That Jack used that heart with impunity was the worst sin of all. Meg stared daggers at his back, knowing this was the last time she would ever see him, the last time he would get anywhere *near* Katie. Meg didn't care if she had to live in the mountains of Tibet. Jack Tarkenton was never going to use her or her daughter again.

Five

Beauty was something Jack had never bothered to define in words. He simply knew it when he saw it, and pursued it wherever he went, be it in the places he lived, the art he collected, the women he kept company with.

But he had never sunk to this level. He had never tried to ruin what he most admired. It was the one thing that allowed him to meet his eyes in the mirror each morning. In spite of his many vices, he had never tried to destroy what he most wanted to have.

Vincent van Gogh was a tortured man. Jack related to the artist's work for that reason. He also found van Gogh's work to be extraordinarily beautiful and complex. Like the woman who stood before him, her ocean eyes lifted to take in what only she could see.

What talent was it that drank in the varied stitches of colors and textures, and understood the artist's vision complete? He wished he knew. If he knew, Meg Masterson Betz would not torture him so. If he knew, he wouldn't have gone after her in the first place.

The medieval tapestry hung in a specially built alcove off the master suite. Isolated by special lighting, the delicate embroidery wove an ancient portrait of a slender, golden-haired princess robed in purple, standing amid a garden of irises, bordered by an ancient coat of arms.

Whatever possessed him to bring her here, to his family's inner sanctum? Did he hope to impress Meg with a masterpiece? Was this exercise in futility all a sop to his pride?

She stood rapt before the tapestry as he knew she would. But Katie was soon bored. She wandered the bedroom adjoining the alcove, playing with the long red ribbons that ran down the front of her dress.

He'd forgotten the family photographs his mother had lined up on the bureau. Framed in silver, they were the exact right height to catch a four-year-old's eye. Katie walked their length and halted before one of the photographs, the one she least needed to see, the one he least wanted to remember.

Of course she picked it up. She looked to her mother first, the question plain on her innocent face, and for the first time in a long time, Jack felt the nakedness of real fear. Was this what it meant to be a father? To make yourself remember what you most wanted to forget?

He laid his hand on her head to reassure her. "Do you know who the man in the picture is, Katie?"

"You," she replied, tilting back to look at him. "'Cept your hair is too brown."

"He's my father, John B. Tarkenton."

She cocked her head in puzzlement. "But he looks the same as you."

"That picture was taken when he was about the same age I am now."

She glanced around the room. "Is this his room?"

"No, Katie. This is my mother's room."

"Where's your daddy's room?"

Jack noted how quickly that question broke Meg's reverie. She hurried over, held her hand out to Katie and smiled gently. "Put the picture back, sweetheart. It's time for us to go now."

"I want to see his daddy's room first," said Katie, taking Jack's hand instead.

Meg sent him a quelling look and drew Katie to the bureau, helping her replace the framed photograph. "Do you remember when I told you about Aunt Amanda's daddy and that he died when she was young? Well, Aunt Amanda and Uncle Jack are brother and sister, and they have the same daddy. He died a long time ago."

Katie slipped her thumb into her mouth. "Did he have an accident?"

"Not like your daddy," Meg said, smoothing Katie's hair. "Not a car accident."

"What kind of accident?" Katie asked around her thumb.

Meg hesitated, searching for words. Jack didn't blame her. He wasn't sure how to explain assassination to a four-year-old, either. But he'd been only a few months older than Katie was now when his father died, and he'd asked the same questions. The adults whispered and his mother cried, and he learned that he shouldn't ask, for no one could bear to tell him the truth.

"More like a people accident, Katie," he said.

Her solemn gaze fastened on him. "What's a people accident?"

Meg knelt beside her. "A bad man shot him, honey."

Katie's eyes widened. "With a gun?"

"Yes," he supplied.

Meg skewered him with one look. Clearly, she didn't want Katie to hear the details. "That's enough, sweetheart. It's time for us to go home."

Careful to keep his expression neutral, Jack followed them from the room. "I wasn't much older than you are now, Katie, when my father died," he offered. "I had just turned five."

"I'm going to be five on my nextest birthday," Katie announced, taking her thumb from her mouth. "My daddy's coming to bring lots of presents."

Meg halted in her tracks. "Your daddy?" she asked, exchanging puzzled looks with Jack.

Katie nodded vigorously. "He's coming down the chimney like Santa."

"Oh, sweetie, no," Meg said, hugging her. "Only Santa comes down chimneys."

Katie turned trusting eyes to Jack. "You believe me, don't you?"

Meg pleaded to him in silent anguish, an anguish he found difficult to ignore. But he couldn't ignore Katie's anguish, either, not when hers was dressed in the unsustainable world of make-believe. "I wanted my dad to come home, too, Katie, after he died. Chimney or the front door, it didn't matter, as long as he came home."

Katie nodded. "I wait by the window so I can see him when he drives up the street. But it's getting darker and darker and sometimes I fall asleep, and he can't come 'less I'm watching.''

"Oh, Katie," Meg exclaimed. "You mustn't believe such things."

"But I have to watch all the time, Mommy. Else he won't come."

Struck by the seriousness of Katie's expression, Jack smoothed her hair back the same way her mother had. "Do you think that's why your daddy died, Katie?" he asked. "Because you weren't watching?"

Clearly startled, Meg gaped at him. But Katie contemplated him with a certain interest, a certain curiosity, placed her thumb back into her mouth and nodded, sucking softly. Meg turned absolutely ashen.

That's when Jack knew why he had brought them here. To punish himself. God knew he needed it. Not only had he abandoned Meg from the start, he hadn't been there for Katie, either.

Careful not to threaten, careful to keep matter-of-fact, he led them to the nearest chair and helped settle Katie on her mother's lap. Crouching below their level, he reached for the right words, the simplest of words. Simple enough for a child to understand.

Meg's watchful mistrust may have been why the words came slowly to him. Or maybe the words came slowly because he had never heard them spoken out loud before. He conjured them out of his own experience, his own memory, his own soul. They were the words he needed to hear but never did, once upon a time, when he was five years old.

"When a person dies, he won't come back, Katie," he began. "That's the hard part about dying. No matter how much your daddy loved you or how much you loved him, he won't ever come back. He can't, you see. That's what being dead means. It's just not possible.''

His voice sounded rusty and hoarse, even to him. That was unusual. He always knew what to say and how to say it, whatever the occasion. That was his special gift, the one inheritance from his father that he appreciated and put to good and frequent use. ''And your daddy didn't die because of you, Katie,'' he continued, taking her tiny hand. ''Nothing you did made him die. That's why it's called an accident. It's no one's fault. The truth is, we all have to die some-time. No one can change that. And no one can bring your daddy back.''

She leaned into the shelter of her mother and stud-ied him, sucking her thumb. She didn't cry. She wasn't ready to cry. She wasn't ready to take it all in, either. She was far too young to have suffered such a tragedy. Unfortunately, that didn't keep trag-edies from happening.

When he ran out of words, he looked to Meg. She took up the slack. She talked about how Katie had her daddy's picture by her bed and that they would always keep him in their memory. She spoke of the church she and Katie went to, of God and family and friends. She said that when Katie missed her daddy especially much, she had her stuffed bunny to hold and her favorite blanket to snuggle under, the one her daddy had touched many times when he tucked her into bed at night.

Meg spoke of all the things Jack didn't know about but should have.

Vincent van Gogh was right. It was much better

to torture yourself rather than inflict it on others. Especially on a child you loved.

Jack insisted on driving them home, arranging for his mother's chauffeur to return Meg's Honda the next morning.

Meg didn't argue. They were past arguing. Katie was the one who mattered most. Emotionally exhausted, she had fallen asleep in Meg's arms.

Jack ran interference, gathering their coats and ordering his car be brought round while Meg made her thank-yous and goodbyes. She declined Bram's offer to drive them home himself and Eleanor's invitation for them to stay the night. Katie needed to sleep in her own house, in her own bed, Meg stated firmly, and she wasn't shy about letting everybody know that she and Jack had some personal issues to discuss during the long drive home.

Reiterating her point, Meg handed Katie over to Jack for the walk outside to the car. He had proved himself tonight, both as parent and ally. To pretend otherwise denied the profoundness of the insight he had shared with Katie.

Following him out to the Jaguar, Meg helped buckle Katie into the back seat. They spoke in tones suitable for a funeral, hushed and grave. Meg conceded it *was* a funeral of sorts, a burial of the bitterness she had felt toward him just a scant hour ago. There was much more to Jack Tarkenton than met the eye.

She studied him in the darkness of the car as he drove the serpentine road, noting the frequency with which he checked the rearview mirror, his concern for Katie evident. No longer was it hard for Meg to believe that this man had been a towheaded little boy in short pants who, some thirty years ago, accepted the American flag that had draped his father's coffin. Jack knew exactly what Katie was going through because he'd been there himself.

He *was* capable of selfless giving, of empathy. She had just been too bitter about their affair to admit it. But admit it Meg did, the moment the car cleared the gates of the estate. "Thank you for what you said to Katie tonight. She obviously needed to hear it."

"I've lost almost five years with her, Meg. I don't want to lose any more. I want us to get married as soon as possible."

Meg flinched at the flatness in his tone. "I concede the pointlessness of sticking by my original conditions," she said carefully. "But I won't dishonor my late husband's memory by considering marriage right now."

"Then when?"

Meg rubbed her temples. The pressure she felt hardly eased. It didn't help when warm, strong fingers reached over and massaged the tightly wrought muscles of her neck. "Don't," she protested.

As usual, he didn't stop. As usual, she felt guilty about how good it felt, how attuned he was to what her body needed, how frightened it made her that he soothed her in exactly the right way. The need to succumb beckoned with its siren's call.

The force of that need brought a terrible ache to her throat. She hated how easily he did this to her, hated the division between her body and her mind. Even if he was willing to make the sacrifices necessary to do right by Katie, falling into his arms was not the answer. Leopards didn't change their spots, and perennial playboys like Jack Tarkenton didn't give up their taste for the fast lane, either.

"Meg? What is it?"

She shook her head, unable to speak past the huge lump in her throat. He was still the same man, all right, the man who had caused her unspeakable heartache. Just because he had a soft spot in his heart for Katie didn't mean he had a soft spot in his heart for anyone else.

Meg swiped her eyes. Quick as it was, it didn't escape his notice. Swearing, he swerved onto the shoulder of the road and stopped the car. She protested, but his hands settled on her shoulders and brought her around to face him.

"Meg, talk to me. What's the matter?"

The dim lights of the dashboard carved shadows into his face, emphasizing the strength of his features. What was she supposed to say? That she was far more attracted to him than to her dear, departed husband? "I can't," she whispered.

"Yes, you can." He tipped her chin up, his fingers cradling her jaw. "After what we went through tonight, you've got to know you can tell me anything."

She squeezed her eyes shut to ward off the intensity of feeling in his eyes, but she could still hear the persuasiveness in his tone and feel the warmth caressing her face.

"You can cry, Meg. It's all right."

Shaking her head, Meg thumped the seat and bit down hard on her knuckles. He was wrong. Crying didn't help. Crying didn't stop the people she loved from being hurt. She didn't want them to feel disappointed in her or betrayed. She didn't want Katie to feel betrayed, either. Katie had been told the most lies of all.

The torrent of agony that thought unleashed had Meg shaking with the grief she should have felt when Allen died. Except Katie was the one Meg truly grieved for. How could she forget all the times Katie waited at the window of the living room, staring out at the street? Or more terrible still, the mornings Meg found her curled on the floor under her bedroom window, fast asleep.

"I should have known," Meg choked out.

"Should have known what?"

"What Katie was going through. She's been looking for Allen all this time, but I didn't know what she was doing. I didn't understand. But I should have. I'm her mother. I should have known."

"Meg, honey, don't do this to yourself. You're a good mother. The best. Even the best can't know everything."

"But—"

"No buts." He swept her damp cheeks with his thumbs, and her chin trembled with the tenderness of the act. "Don't forget, Meg. You were grieving, too."

"No," Meg cried. "You don't understand." She caught the open sides of his jacket, bunching it in her fists. She was always so afraid of letting the truth slip, of dropping more than his name, of revealing how well she really knew Jack Tarkenton. "Don't you see?" she cried. "Everything is a lie."

Gathering her to his chest, he held her head against the comforting hardness of his shoulder. "Not everything, Meg. Not Katie. If you hadn't been there to make her feel safe, she never would have opened up tonight.''

"I'd give my last breath to save her from any more pain.''

"I know, babe.'' His voice broke. "Me, too.''

Moved by the hot feel of his tears, Meg drew back and reached with her fingertips, finding moisture under his eyes. Holding her hand up into the slicing headlights of passing cars, she rubbed the gleam of moisture between forefinger and thumb.

He captured her hand and laid it alongside his face, his palm pressing her knuckles with a tenderness that took her breath. Staring into his eyes, she wondered at the haunting guilt and concern she saw there. Or was it a trick of the shifting and ghostly light?

He kissed her softly on the lips. She should have stopped herself then, stopped herself from seeking such solace. Or seeking to give it, especially to him. With Jack, there was no such thing as solace. There was only the taste of their tears, salt-warm and natural, as natural as the hunger that opened her mouth to his.

Cradling her head, he sampled her tongue with long, deep strokes. Her sense of urgency grew. She speared fingers through his thick hair, giving as good as she got, desire stealing what remained of her sense. Until she remembered...

"Katie,'' she gasped. "Jack, stop. We can't. Not with Katie here.''

He froze. "Is she awake?''

Meg pulled away from him and peered into the shadowy backseat. "No, thank goodness.''

Jack straightened behind the steering wheel and

raked both hands through his hair. "I can't believe this. We were necking like a couple of teenagers."

"This can't happen again."

"Agreed. Not until we're married, at least. So when is the happy day going to be?"

"I told you before. I will not discuss this, Jack."

"We have a child," he said doggedly and jammed the car into gear, as if trying to muscle it back on the highway. "We have an attraction strong enough to produce that child. It's a start."

It was certainly more of a start than she and Allen had. Guilty at the thought, Meg bit her lip. But why should love matter so much? She hadn't been in love with Allen when she married him. What if she did give in to Jack's proposal?

The prospect weakened Meg's knees.

The memories assaulted her. Memories of the first time they met, the first time they came together, the first time they made love. At least she believed it was love. In his arms, she had felt so cherished, special, beyond compare.

The vividness of her recollection reminded her that she and Jack did have something going for them. But sexual chemistry only went so far, especially when it came to marriage. Love didn't come from sharing a bed. Eventually he'd tire of her like he did before— like he did with every woman he showed an interest in. Inevitably, he would move on to someone else. And Meg knew she wasn't the type who could turn a blind eye to immoral behavior. Otherwise saying yes to his proposal would be an empty gesture, and the vows they would make to each other would be empty, too.

For the hundredth time, Meg wished she knew

Jack better. Except she did know him. Every time she got within two feet of him, her pounding heart reminded her of how well. And she couldn't forget he was the one who got Katie to talk tonight, to confess the wishes in her hopeful little heart. He asked the hard questions, the right questions. And he was her biological father.

Meg closed her eyes and leaned back against the headrest of the car, praying for guidance, praying to do what was right.

His life was an open book. Every talk show host in America had interviewed him at one time or another. He'd been endlessly dissected and analyzed by every psychological and political hack on radio and TV. Most called him clever and cagey, citing his quest to circumvent the expectations that came with the Tarkenton name as understandable, considering the enormity of his father's contributions to the world. The paparazzi certainly never let him get away with a thing.

"What's it going to take, Meg?" he asked. "I promise to be there for Katie no matter what. You and I will stand together as her parents. Commitments don't get much more serious than that."

"I need to see more of you and Katie together."

"You have seen us together. You'll see more over the next few weeks."

"Good grief," she burst out. "Do we have to decide our entire future tonight?"

"Time is of the essence." He glanced back at Katie and lowered his voice. "People are already talking about us."

"If you hadn't opened your big mouth, your family wouldn't suspect a thing."

"I'm not talking about my family. I'm talking about gossips and reporters. My office has already fielded calls about our relationship. Rumors are circulating on the street that we are definitely an item."

"How can that be? Who else could possibly know?"

"It's not what people know. It's what they assume and what they manufacture in order to sell newspapers. Remember when Bram and I picked you and Katie up at her day care center? Somebody there tipped the media. The calls started the next day."

"You ambushed me there on purpose. You wanted this to happen. You made this happen."

"The tabloid press is a reality, Meg. Whether we get married in two years or two months, you'll have to learn to deal with it."

"Me? What about you? You're the one who started this!"

"Is that going to be your attitude when the paparazzi turn their cameras on Katie? She's going to be as much a victim as you are."

"How am I supposed to explain this to her? I can't justify getting married to you right now to myself, much less to any one else. People are going to think I'm pregnant and we had to get married."

"Time will take care of that rumor. As for our decision to marry sooner rather than later, all you have to do is say what I'm going to say: Because of the close family ties between the Tarkentons and the Mastersons, you and I have known each other for a long time. When Allen died, it was natural for me, given my own experience with the death of a loved one, to offer my help and support. But our friendship turned into something more."

"You should be a politician. You can rationalize anything."

"It's a gift that runs in my family."

But Meg wondered how could she ever trust what he said when he could manipulate the truth so easily. "Your gift is one I don't particularly like," she told him.

He chuckled. "Don't worry. You'll come to appreciate it more and more as time goes by."

"No, I won't. Look, Jack, drop the idea of us getting married any time soon. It's not going to happen."

"No, you look," he retorted, his cavalier attitude gone. "You're right about my wild reputation, especially where women are concerned. Couple that with the truth about how Katie was conceived and we've got a time bomb on our hands. I can't protect either one of you without benefit of marriage. It gives me the power to seek legal recourse if some reporter sticks his nose where it doesn't belong."

"If someone gets wind of the truth, legal recourse is going to be the least of our problems. Besides, even John B. Tarkenton Jr. isn't rich enough to sue everybody."

"I won't have to. I know how these media people operate. If you and I work together, we can string them along, make them believe anything we want. We have to live under the same roof to do it, though. Now, I don't know about you, but I think our living together is going to be a whole lot easier to explain to Katie and our families if you're wearing a wedding ring."

"I'm already wearing a wedding ring. See?" She flashed her left hand.

"You're a widow, Meg."

"Can't you get it through your thick head? Allen's barely cold in his grave!"

"You loved your husband. I understand."

Meg opened her mouth to refute him, but at this point, she certainly wasn't about to engage Jack in a discussion about the finer points of her marriage to Allen. "How would you feel if I threw this back at you?" she demanded. "What if I said *you* have to completely change how you live *your* life. No more women. No more parties. No more expensive toys. No more jetting around whenever and wherever you want. For once in your life, you'll have to consider the feelings of someone else, namely me."

"Interesting proposition."

"I'm serious."

"So am I. Are you saying you want fidelity? You've got it. As my wife, you can expect me to be a model husband. I'll even give you veto power over all my travel arrangements. Satisfied?"

"Separate bedrooms."

He shot her a glance. "Is that what we're negotiating now? Sleeping arrangements? Certainly you don't expect us to remain celibate for the rest of our lives."

She didn't bat an eye. "I'm not making any promises. You'll have to find a job, too."

"Meg," he reminded her gently. "I have an office in the city."

"There's a difference between a job and an office. I won't have you hanging around my house all day."

"Your house?" He hooted. "You can't seriously believe I'd live in the suburbs of New Jersey."

"Why not? It's a nice, quiet neighborhood filled with nice, quiet people."

Unwilling to enter the territory of nice and quiet, much less explain why he didn't want to live in the house she had shared with Mr. Perfect Husband, Jack changed the subject. "It's the media, Meg. They'll swarm the place. They can't be ignored."

"A few weeks of nice and quiet should take care of that problem."

"We can live anywhere in the world, anywhere you want," he offered. "You won't have to work, won't have to lift a finger."

"I happen to like working. I happen to like living in the suburbs of New Jersey, too."

Jack cursed under his breath. "Then I *do* want to hang around with Katie the three days a week you commute into the city. I want to have that time with her."

"She likes her day-care place and she likes coming into the city with me."

"She'll like her time with me better. Now, the only point of contention is the date of the wedding."

"That's not true and you know it."

"What's not true? You accepted my proposal. You waived your conditions on it. We agree that Katie must be protected at all costs. I'll concede the point that she should keep Allen's name. There's no greater tribute to a father than that. What more do you want?"

"For you to stop rushing me!"

"Suppose your sainted Allen had to make a choice between running the risk of offending people or exposing Katie to possible harm? Which would he choose?"

Meg said a very inelegant word, in French no less, which only served to make him switch to French, too. Meg shut out the eloquence of his message but that didn't stop her from remembering he had performed the very same feat when they first met. His fluency impressed her as much now as it did then. Jack knew how to use every persuasive language there was, sensual and otherwise.

She thought she had learned how to answer him. She'd run out of answers tonight.

Six

Meg searched Jack's determined profile in the dimness of the Jaguar. "What will we tell our families?" she asked.

"The truth." He shrugged. "We're getting married on New Year's Day."

"In six weeks? They won't believe it."

"Then we'll have to make them believe it, won't we? A kiss here, a caress there..."

He flashed his patented grin her way, the devil smiling in his eyes. She bit back her own devil and confessed her biggest worry. "You've hardly spent any time with Katie. She won't be fooled."

"Children never are. Developmentally, her age gives us a little leeway. Fairy tales are as true to her as real life. She'll see her mother kiss the frog and believe that you and I will live happily ever after."

The smug authority in his voice irritated Meg. "Since when do you know so much about raising children?"

"I admit I don't have your sterling credentials. J.J.'s been an education, though."

"Girls are a lot different from boys."

"I'll be sure to look to you for advice. After we're married, that is."

Married. Had she actually agreed to it? "I have another condition."

"And what might that be?"

"I want a justice of the peace," Meg said quietly. "Only family will attend."

"I want the ceremony at the estate, in order to keep it as private as possible. And I want Katie there."

"She's family, isn't she?"

"Yours, not mine. Betz is her last name, remember? Allen will always officially be her father."

Later, Meg was to ponder why Jack was so adamant. But that was the one promise that gave her the most comfort. In many ways, Jack was an honorable man.

Meg wrestled with the meaning of her own honor the following week, when she ducked into Bloomingdale's to shop for a wedding dress.

She started in the Career Woman Department, looking for something in knee-length ivory, classy and dressy enough for evening. Problem was, she already owned such a dress. She'd worn it the first time around, when she married Allen.

Marrying as soon as possible had been *the* priority then. Unable to splurge, she stitched faux pearls on the bodice of her whitest dress. Hours later, they came out of the courthouse after a five-minute ceremony. Family and friends weren't told until after the fact.

At least this time, her mother and siblings would be in attendance. But just as before, there were no invitations. Invitations would tip the media, as would the inclusion of bridesmaids and groomsmen. In fact, too much was just like before, including the dresses she was looking at.

Meg wandered on to Evening Attire, feeling alone and out of place. If she weren't so pressed for time, she could have used her designer contacts to come up with something original. The world of fashion was not the place to keep secrets, however. With all the rumors flying around about her and Jack Tarkenton, Meg didn't want to be asked why she needed a cream-colored suit whipped together by New Year's Day.

She had yet to talk to him about New Year's resolutions, but she would, though, and soon. Already there was speculation about whether he was faithful to her, and the idea of his cheating bothered her more and more.

Was that why she chose a sexy floor-length gown, thin as gossamer and white as fresh-fallen snow? The significance of the virginal color would not be lost on him, either. If nothing else, Meg respected his intelligence. And wasn't it perfectly natural for the bride to want fidelity from the groom?

She justified the outrageous cost of the dress by telling herself she'd wear it again and again. Jack had already put her on notice that he expected her to accompany him to various charity balls and fund-raisers. The Tarkentons were widely known for their many philanthropic interests.

Recalling the probable recognition that went with those interests, Meg plunked down her credit card. If Jack wanted her by his side, she wasn't going to fade into the woodwork. She would make a statement all her own.

Accordingly, she refused to buy a veil or even a hat. She refused to wear his diamond engagement ring, either. His secretary ended up ordering their wedding bands through a catalog. Simple bands of gold, they were identical in every way except size, and were shipped to a post office box registered to another name. The subterfuge was necessary, again because of the media.

With her wearing pristine white, Meg chose pink taffeta for her daughter. The color of the dresses was her only concession to convention. She planned to enter this marriage with her eyes open and her head uncovered. This time around, she wasn't harboring any illusions.

"I now pronounce you man and wife. You may kiss the bride."

Jack kissed her as if their union was a love match. There were a lot of people they needed to fool. His best man was one of them. Bram glowered throughout the ceremony. Jack saw what it did to Meg. He also saw what happened when he kissed her.

Flustered was not the right word. Meg was too regal to get flustered. Color regained, she turned on her heel and took his arm. That's when he realized how shaky his bride truly was. Her death grip made him feel more like her husband than the vows did.

Katie led the way down the aisle formed by rows of chairs set in the formal living room, dropping little pink flower petals from a miniature basket. Meg's mother and his met their procession at the archway to the dining room, misty-eyed but smiling proudly, and started the receiving line. Standing amidst the lot of them, he was outnumbered by females four to one.

His sense of suffocation worsened as the day progressed. It was all the things he was giving up. The nightlife, the women, the freedom to come and go when he pleased.

The dress Meg wore didn't help. She had poured herself into a vaselike shape of shimmering white, flawless and fair like her skin, the whole crowned by the cloud of her hair.

He couldn't wait to sink his hands into it.

He'd take the time necessary to bring her willingly to their bed. But he would have her there and soon. He was her husband, dammit, and she was his wife.

During the reception, he touched her in small ways, in discreet places. She pretended not to notice. If he looked closely, though, he spotted the telltale signs of arousal. The dress was a simple slip of a thing, designed to show every curve of her slender figure.

Ridiculous as the idea was, Jack arranged a honeymoon. Ridiculous because Meg had rejected the idea out of hand. Her best argument concerned Katie. Even one night was one night too long to be away from her.

Jack agreed. But their families didn't know why

that was true. Neither did the media. They would think it strange if he didn't stage some sort of an escape with his bride. So he arranged for Katie to spend the night with Amanda and Bram, and made reservations at the very new and exclusive Hotel Coventry.

There was always a chance once he got Meg alone, he'd overcome her scruples. She had the heart of a romantic. He knew the art of romance well. That's how he first introduced himself to her, in fact.

Arriving at the rehearsal dinner for his sister's wedding late as usual, he did his customary scoping for the best looking women in the crowd. Through the din of the crowd, he heard a distinctive female voice speaking French.

Intrigued, he moved in behind her, overhearing the obscure but excellent French wine she ordered in the accent of a native. The moment the waiter left, Jack whispered a rather bawdy French joke in her ear. She turned to see who would say such a naughty thing, eyes merry. The rest of her was pure Paris couture.

They traded witty repartee until dinner was called. By then he had discovered who she was. Meg Masterson, sister to his soon-to-be brother-in-law. Marguerite, as she was called in French, currently lived on the Upper West side of New York city, had talent enough to have graduated from the Sorbonne, and a mind quick enough to pick up nuances.

He maneuvered his way into being her dinner partner. She was flattered, he could tell. Her eyes sparkled when he seated her. She even flirted. Only later would he realize she did it rather artlessly. But he'd been drinking very heavily in those days, and he encouraged her to drink more.

With his obligation to toast the impending nuptials done with, he wooed her away from family and friends. They strolled the grounds of the hotel where the wedding party was staying, talking. The night was cool enough for her to take his coat and the shadows deep enough to disguise their path, and though it taxed his skills of discretion, he seduced her to his room.

Once they got there, it felt as if she won in the wild rush that followed. Won a contest, a duel, one where he made the rules. He broke them with her that night, the only time in his life when he wasn't careful or controlled, and Katie was conceived.

He had wanted Meg that badly.

Far too enamored for his own good, he decided to kill his lust for the lovely young woman when he woke at dawn the next morning to find her still in his bed.

He roused her in slow degrees, dedicated to proving that the previous night had simply been a lesson in the recklessness of too much drink in too little time.

He didn't confess what he was up to other than to whisper that he wanted to see her in the early morning light, for she was like the finest sculpture to him, irresistible to the touch and priceless in her perfection.

Such words came easily because he said them often. Women rewarded such flattery. Meg was no different. But that morning he discovered she was far less sophisticated than he thought.

He measured the way they came together, judging the fit of their bodies, watching how she moved and he moved, and fell under her spell once again, discovering the art of their very special dance.

When she left, sneaking out to her own room, he wanted to follow. He wanted to have her all over again. Until he saw traces of fresh blood on the sheets. That's when he realized how truly infatuated he was. He had missed all the signs, ignored all the signals the uninitiated usually sent out.

That's why he lured her back to his room the next night. He could not believe she was a virgin. She had to be faking it. There had to be subterfuge behind that dark and cosmopolitan beauty, that continental flair.

Planning to test his theory with a quick bout of unadulterated, raw sex, he captured her bodily the moment she entered his room. Shutting the door, he pinned her against it. But she put shy hands on his chest and lifted her face to be kissed, and he knew what he had suspected was true even while he denied it.

He found himself teasing her, rubbing her soft, full lips, and there wasn't anything raw about it.

It was Saturday, the wedding day, and she still wore her bridesmaid's dress. Deep teal in color, it swathed her from her neck to the tips of her dyed-to-match shoes. He skimmed his hands down her sides, the delicacy of curves enhanced by the slip-slide of silk against lace.

She wore the most famous and beloved of French perfumes behind her ears, on her wrists and between her breasts. That he already had discovered. But it wasn't until he turned her around and unzipped her dress that he learned she perfumed the back of her neck as well.

Breathing deeply, he let the dress fall and whispered words of enticement to her, the usual words. Only she quivered when she heard them. He had to close his eyes to cut off the sight, to keep from taking her right then and there.

Perhaps that was why he scooped her into his arms and carried her to his bed. Until Meg, he had never made the mistake of carrying a woman to his bed before. Certainly he hadn't since.

With her settled against the pillows, he kicked off his shoes, stripped off his tie. Studs flew with the shedding of his shirt, and he hooked his briefs along with his trousers, sliding them down together. Suddenly shy, she shuttered her eyes.

He should have been angry. Instead, he thought how precious she was and used her shyness as an excuse to slow down.

By then he knew the sacrifices she had made for the sake of her art. She worked with her hands, so her nails were cut short and straight across, and he wanted to feel how she shaped and created in the pursuit of her passion.

He slid his hand beneath the small of her back, hearing the rustle of taffeta against satin, feeling the seams and subtle abrasions of lace underneath. The delicate lingerie he drew off her yesterday came to mind, especially the triangle of black silk that led him where he most wanted to go.

The texture did something to her, adding to her experience of pleasure. He brushed the nest of lace with the heel of his hand, then fingered her, and her eyes begged. "Please," she gasped.

"Please what?"

"Free me."

He did, slipping the lace down her legs. Yet when he locked his gaze with hers and eased his way in, the color of her eyes changed with each move he made, as the color of van Gogh's paintings changed with the light. Only with her, it was life he saw, life that changed.

He tried to go back. He tried to recapture his jaded youth. He tried to prove she wasn't the cause of his listless days and sleepless nights. He certainly told himself otherwise. He showed it by not calling her as promised, resorting to aimlessly traveling the world, performing every act imaginable and unimaginable with the constant stream of women he took, satiating an insatiable need.

Drowning himself, in the end, in a den of iniquities.

Meg laced her hands together nervously. Their going-away limousine was chilly. Blessedly so. Thank heavens for January, for winter, for the icy pall that reduced her wedding day to the dull look of the ordinary.

For it *was* ordinary. It had to be. However formal and formidable Jack looked in black tie and tails, he didn't mean a word of the vows he had said. Yet, as he settled next to her in the limo's leather back seat, the elegance of his body edged her peripheral vision as it had throughout the day, and the pounding of her heart refused to cease.

Cleave unto him.

The width of his powerful shoulders, the bend of his lean, black-clad legs belonged to the man she married. And those vows repeated themselves over and over in her mind.

I now pronounce you man and wife...

Clearing the gates of the Tarkenton estate, the limousine turned east, surrounded by a contingent of motorcycle police. Meg glanced at the caravan of reporters who took up the chase, snaking behind in a long line of jockeying cars and satellite vans.

Jack checked on them, too. Hair the color of sand fanned his collar. Sea-spice aftershave sent visions of sunlit beaches through her head. Deserted beaches. Deserted except for one man and one woman. Her husband, his wife.

"Don't worry," he said, and clasped her hand. "The hotel has plenty of security."

She nodded, too aware of his hand, his voice, of *now and forever, amen.*

She looked ahead, taking in the reality of snow-banked roads and frozen trees. A nearby hotel was their destination, not Saint-Tropez. However, what remained on her mind was the stripe of his shirt collar against the strong cords of his neck. His very tanned neck. Five years ago, she discovered exactly where that tan ended, too.

Appalled at the direction of her thoughts, Meg concentrated on Katie, sweet and innocent. Katie came from somewhere, though. Katie came from *him.*

Heat flushed Meg. She pulled her hand out from under his and placed it in her lap, trying to make light of the situation. After all, it was ironic. She had been so worried about Jack coming on to her. But deep in her heart, she didn't find the situation humorous at all. Deep in her heart, Meg wondered if she lived by her word, if she honored her vows, if she stood as morally upright as she believed.

Does this woman take this man...

Or maybe she was simply succumbing to the devil inside and rationalizing beyond belief.

She was *not* sleeping with him. They had already discussed the parameters of their relationship. Sharing a hotel room was merely a cover for the press. Jack wasn't expecting a thing.

He didn't suspect a thing, either.

Meg wished he did. She wished he knew exactly how difficult he was making this for her by virtue of his sheltering hand and husky voice and the power of his masculine presence. Then he'd be the one with the problem on his hands. Knowing Jack, though, he wouldn't see it as a problem.

Desperate now, she pictured Allen, searching for a literal dash of cold water on her senses. A dash of cold water against a rising Atlantic tide.

The clean, modern lines of the hotel came into view, and the limousine swung off the boulevard. More police lay in wait and closed off the parade of press vehicles, creating a barricade against the blitzkrieg lights and shouts for attention.

Ignoring the din, Jack helped her out of the car and shepherded her through a gauntlet of applauding hotel staff into the relative quiet calm of new world elegance.

The hotel's spectacular lobby proved to be the distraction Meg needed. Restful in hues of ecru, amber and olive green, it exuded a subdued atmosphere that invited her to take a deep and fortifying breath. She even met Jack's inquiring lift of his brow with a genuine smile.

"That was quite a welcome. Are you all right?" he asked.

"Fine, thanks."

The long look they exchanged turned her reply into an absolute lie. Her knees weakened, and the time it took to check in and for the elevator to rise to the top floor churned more butterflies. Grateful for the bellboy who chaperoned them, Meg studied the white satin toes of her shoes.

The elevator doors slid apart and she stepped out first, all too conscious of the two men behind her. The bellboy bounded ahead and unlocked the bridal suite door, and suddenly she was swept off her feet.

With one supporting arm at her back and one cradling the crook of her knees, Jack grinned down at her. "Don't look so surprised, Mrs. Tarkenton. It's a tradition," he said, and carried her over the threshold.

He already had the bellboy's tip in his hand. The bellboy delivered their luggage and saluted smartly before closing the door behind him. Immediately Jack set her down, going so far as to apologize for taking such liberties.

"Jack, please," Meg protested, thinking of the flannel pajamas she'd packed, of the hardbacks she'd brought, planning to use the books like barricades if he dared get too close.

"You're afraid of me, aren't you," he asked with the most rueful expression on his face.

"Of course not."

"I really can't blame you. I've given you reason to be." He tucked her hand into the crook of his elbow, escorting her farther into the suite. "The reason I wanted to come here, to have a wedding night," he said, "was to prove that the two of us can be alone together without me taking advantage of you."

Before Meg had a chance to shut her open mouth, he left her and disappeared into the adjoining room, whistling and shrugging off his jacket.

Her insane impulse to follow had Meg pacing the suite like a caged tiger. Decorated in pastels and white-washed woods, the room surrounded her with understated style and taste. Unfortunately, she could have been in a budget motel for all she cared. The bedroom occupied her thoughts. And what was he doing in there? Changing his clothes, most likely.

She checked her own dress, making sure every zipper was zipped, every strap was in place, and caught herself wishing she had changed into something more comfortable. *Much* more comfortable.

Face flaming, she plunked herself in the nearest chair, switched on the television and pushed the remote buttons until she found CNN. Fires and catastrophes loomed large. Across the world, people faced crises of terrible proportions, and here she sat, twisting her brand-new ring, behaving like an ninny.

She heard him return, still whistling. The most absurd apprehension nailed her to the chair. What if he wasn't wearing anything? Considering some of the stunts he'd pulled with her, she wouldn't put it past him.

"Are you a news junkie?" he asked from behind her.

"I like to keep up with what's going on," she admitted.

"Me, too." He asked a background question about the lead story. She sneaked a glance at him when she answered and relief flooded her. He hadn't changed clothes at all. The only thing missing was his jacket. Cuff links, too. He'd rolled up his sleeves. Once she noted the corded muscles of his forearms, she quickly refastened her gaze on the TV.

"What time would you like to eat?" he asked.

"Eat?"

"Food, sustenance, the bread of life. The hotel has a five-star restaurant that comes highly recommended."

She deliberated. Nonexistent though her appetite was, the idea of being surrounded by a room full of other people appealed to her. There was safety in numbers. She certainly wasn't going to tear off his clothes if people were watching. She wasn't that far gone.

Yet.

Jumping to her feet, she said in her briskest manner, "Give me half an hour."

"Certainly."

Thus committed, she slipped into the bedroom to get ready. An expansive bouquet of long-stemmed white roses lay on the king-size bed. Not daring to ask, she hoped the flowers were supplied by the hotel. This was the bridal suite, after all.

She saw he had unpacked. His tuxedo jacket hung in the closet, along with a more casual herringbone tweed. Next to it hung a pressed shirt and khaki slacks. Cordovan loafers were neatly lined up on the closet floor. Seeing his clothes brought it all home to her.

And thereto I pledge thee my troth.

Forcing the memory of those words from her mind, Meg made short work of emptying her overnight bag and opened the other side of the closet. She gasped, and her armful of clothes tumbled to the floor. More roses, tiny and scarlet this time, lay scattered on the top shelf. The question of who had placed them so strategically was answered. Jack. What remained was the question of why.

He wasn't above manipulating her with a romantic gesture or two. She knew that.

Congratulating herself on the soundness of the insight, Meg put away her clothes and bustled into the bathroom. Laid across the shiny marble sink was a single long-stemmed yellow rose. A card was attached. *For my wife, Meg,* the distinctive handwriting read.

She stared for an endless moment, then picked up the rose and touched the fragrance to her nose, the feel of petals to her lips, moist and sweet.

Of all the memories they shared, this one remained best remembered, of roses traced upon her skin, of tasting the crush of petals on him. Perhaps he had experienced the same thing with some other woman in some other time. His smile had been lazy at first. But in the end, face-to-face and body-to-body, with nothing between them but the most sensitive of skin, the depths of his eyes had splintered, and she fancied she saw love there.

Youth fancied many things, she discovered. But an unborn child brought such fantasies immediately down to earth. When she learned she was pregnant, her first thought was to call Jack immediately. But if the truth hadn't been obvious before, it was by then. The father of her child just wasn't father material. Despite his many promises and the intensity of their passion, he hadn't bothered to follow up with so much as a phone call.

Now a slim band of gold weighed heavy on her hand. She had always believed in promises. That is, until Jack came along.

For better or worse...

She might not believe his promises, but she had always kept her own. She might not have the feelings of a new bride, but that didn't make Jack any less her husband. She had given him her word *from this day forward...*

Meg stared at her reflection in the bathroom mirror, seeing the nervous blanching of her skin. However noble her intentions, she was not a saint. She couldn't pretend to love a man even if she was married to him. Her experience with Allen proved it. Either the feeling was there to begin with, as with Amanda and Bram, or the feeling didn't exist at all.

Shaking herself from her reverie, Meg hid her cosmetic bag in one of the bathroom drawers. Jack, on the other hand, had a little more faith about revealing his personal items. Stored in a corner by the sink was his leather shaving kit. She battled a most human urge to peek inside it.

And all my worldly goods with thee I share.

She returned her cosmetic bag to the counter, then switched it from one side of the sink to the other, seeing her foolishness and feeling it, too, but the agony of indecision didn't end. And it had nothing to do with worldly goods.

With my body, I thee honor…

The truth was, she didn't know what the future held. Allen's sudden death had taught her that. Maybe if she gave in tonight to the intense attraction she felt for Jack, they might uncover feelings enough to make a future. To not try to fulfill her promises, to not give the marriage her all… *now and forever, amen.*

Jack claimed he wanted to earn her trust. Problem was, he already had it. She wasn't afraid to trust him. She was afraid to trust herself.

Seven

Determined to act upon her wedding vows, Meg carried the single rose with her into the living area of the suite. Jack lounged on the couch in front of the television, the picture of relaxed formality in his tux, a copy of the *Wall Street Journal* on his lap.

"Thank you," she said, lifting the rose.

"You're welcome." He switched off the television and folded the newspaper. "I wanted to do something special."

"You did." Gathering her courage to take the initiative, Meg perched on the chair opposite him. "What would you think about ordering room service? I think I've had enough of people tonight."

"I couldn't agree more." With a smile, he passed her the leather-bound menu. "Room service it is."

Meg pored over it, supremely self-conscious. But

it wasn't as though she had invited him to jump into bed with her. They had to dine, and now that she had time to think about it, to do so in front of a room full of gawking strangers held little appeal. Especially if she wanted to engage her new husband in meaningful and intimate conversation.

To set the right mood for the meal, she chose Chateaubriand for two, which appeared to please him. He made the required phone call, leaving Meg to wait in the chair, wondering what to do next. Her palms were already damp. She smoothed them over the upholstery, telling herself not to be nervous, that she had only committed herself to sharing a private meal with him. The first order of business was to simply relax.

When he returned, they talked of Katie, of how well she was adjusting despite the overwhelming press coverage that came with the announcement of their nuptials. Luckily, very little of the coverage had focused on her. Instead, as Meg had predicted, the media fixated on speculating about how she and Jack could possibly have fallen in love so quickly, especially when she was supposedly grieving the recent loss of her husband.

Their prepared statements satisfied some of the less ferocious of the media while serving, also, to put to rest any doubts expressed by their families. Any openly expressed doubts, at least.

Further rescue came from an unexpected quarter. A well-known gossip columnist for one of the newspapers suggested that what really motivated Jack Tarkenton's abrupt decision to wed was his deep psychological need to get over the trauma of his childhood. The tragic figure of a recent widow like Meg couldn't help but reawaken memories of his own mother going through the same thing. Suggesting that he had an Oedipal complex, the columnist opined that since Jack and Meg were related by marriage that made her the perfect candidate. She was vulnerable to his pursuit because of her grief and need to provide for her youngster.

Even though she and Jack had shared a laugh over that one, Meg remembered wondering if there might be a kernel of truth in such musings. But she'd made sure she did a good job of ignoring it all, and had concentrated instead on making the holiday season a special one for Katie. Between the excitement of Christmas and the secret planning of the wedding, the time had been hectic for all of them. Now that it was behind them, Meg and Jack were able to relax and make friendly small talk.

A small army of waiters, discreetly uniformed in black vests and tuxedo pants, wheeled in three trolley carts, setting an elegant table for two in red linens. Centered in the forest of china and crystal was a silver domed platter. Dispatching the group with the stroke of a pen, Jack waited until they left, then pulled out a chair, insisting on seating Meg himself.

"Wine, Madame?" he asked, displaying the bottle over his arm.

Meg did a double-take over the distinctive French label. Chateau Gruand-Larose Saint-Julien. Even the year was correct. "You remembered," she exclaimed, glancing up at him in total surprise.

He gave her an indulgent smile and splashed her

glass with the ruby bordeaux. "Why wouldn't I remember? It was the night we first met."

"Jack," she reminded him, "we met more than five years ago."

"I remember everything about that night," he claimed, taking his seat and filling his own glass.

"Really?" A teasing dimple dented her cheek. "I find that difficult to believe."

"Test me then."

She picked up her glass and sipped thoughtfully, ebony lashes demure against her high-boned cheeks. "Do you remember where we met?"

"At the rehearsal dinner for Amanda and Bram's wedding—The Four Fountains Restaurant, to be precise."

"Even I didn't remember the name of the restaurant."

"I told you. I remember everything."

"What was I wearing?"

He didn't miss a beat. "Black panties."

She sputtered and threw her napkin at him.

Jack lofted it back with a smile. "You wore a silk sheathe, very Parisian. The color was royal blue. You told me you bought it from a shop on rue Cambon. That's when we gave up all pretense and decided to speak in the language of love."

"Was that what it was?" she asked lightly. "Love?"

He chuckled, unwilling to risk the mood with too frank an answer. "The French certainly think they speak the language of love. It's their major claim to fame."

"I know some curators at Versailles or the Louvre

who might take issue with that. Tell me, do you travel much to France?''

"Enough to keep fluent. You?''

"Last year I went for the first time since school, for the designer shows.'' She traced the rim of her wineglass, suddenly pensive. "I miss France. Especially Paris.''

"Of course. Paris. Why didn't I think of it before? It's the perfect place for a honeymoon. We'll catch the Concorde tomorrow.''

"To Paris?'' she asked, obviously startled.

He lifted his wineglass, toasting her. "Your wish, my dear wife, is my command.''

"But, we can't go to Paris.''

"Why not, Meg? You love Paris.''

"What about Katie? We're supposed to pick her up tomorrow.''

Meg had a point. "We'll take her with us,'' he said.

"Jack, she's four years old. What will she do there?''

"We'll hire a nanny. She'll have a great time.''

"On our so-called honeymoon? I'm sure the media will have nothing good to say about that.''

"Fine,'' he clipped. "We won't go to Paris.'' He stabbed at his meat, put off by his own annoyance. He shouldn't care if they went or not.

"Perhaps we can go next year, when Katie's older. For our first wedding anniversary.''

Somewhat mollified, he covered her hand. "I'll hold you to that.''

To his amazement, she held his gaze for a long

moment, the curl of her fingers pliant beneath his. "I know you will."

He raised her hand to his lips and sealed the promise with a kiss. Withdrawing her hand with a smile, she resumed eating, and sipped her wine with graceful poise. But he sensed how much remained hidden behind her outward show of composure. To encourage her to relax even more, he refilled their wineglasses and plied her with questions about Katie, about the times he missed since the day she'd been born.

Answering patiently, Meg handled her silverware in deft European style, the knife in her right hand and eating from the fork in her left, relishing the meal and the wine in the same way he was. He had always admired her stylish yet winsome manner, making her appear both sophisticated and approachable at the same time. From the moment they met, he had been taken with her. By storm.

He asked her about her work. The fashion industry attracted all sorts of characters, and Meg described them in vivid yet respectful terms, especially the sometimes eccentric weavers who were working with her to preserve the old ways of making the wools, silks and satins that replicated the most historically celebrated fabrics on earth.

The musicality of her voice didn't distract him, however, from the allure of her body, showcased to perfection by her wedding gown.

Halfway through their second bottle of wine, one of his wryer comments made her laugh. Shaking with mirth, she collapsed back in her chair, giggling behind her napkin.

Tempted to join her, he held himself back, thinking he had to be very careful in building her trust and handling the sense of camaraderie developing between them. One wrong move, and he'd be banished to the couch, sentenced to sleeping alone not only tonight but many more to come. There were certain steps he had to take in order to entice her into bed. That knowledge gained him a considerable amount of control, and he raised his wineglass in another toast. "To new beginnings."

She clinked her glass against his. "To ours."

He watched her while she savored the wine, feeling the growing furnace in his belly. He ended up draining his glass just to keep focused. "Magnifique."

He had the distinct pleasure of seeing a delicate shade of rose blossom on her cheeks. "You're spoiling me."

"Really?" He pushed away from the table. "Come here, Meg."

She rose and halted before him. Amazed she'd obeyed without question, he linked fingers with hers, encouraging her tentative smile.

Lord, he was tempted to pull her down into his lap. But he wasn't about to let the rapport he'd worked so hard to establish between them slip away. "Are you ready for dessert?"

"Aren't you?"

"I thought you wanted to wait." Ready to pounce, he counted his heartbeat instead, annoyed by its speed. He didn't want her to guess what her nearness did to him.

"I don't know," she mused and wound a lock of

his hair around her finger. ''Isn't it a woman's prerogative to change her mind?''

It was. And there was no clearer signal than her smile and the urgency it brought him. But the ease in which she had given in nagged at him. Meg wasn't one to change her mind, not without a good reason. ''What are you saying?'' he asked cautiously.

''Come now, Jack. Isn't it obvious? I want to do what all newlyweds do on their wedding night.''

She knelt at his feet, the picture of bridal devotion. Yet her hands fisted tight, the knuckles stark and white when she placed them on his thighs, as if she was offering herself to him like some sacrificial lamb.

Maybe she was. And he shouldn't be surprised. If he'd learned one thing about Meg in the years since they met, it was the extent of her virtue. Unfortunately, his sense of virtue didn't extend nearly as far.

He stroked her face like a blind man might, seeking the structure beneath, the strength of form softened by silk, only alive. She closed her eyes, and he smoothed the line of her brows with his thumbs, soothing her worries. He didn't want to take advantage of her. But her fists remained tensed and stoic on his thighs.

He wove fingers through her hair, letting it curl around his palms and fall back into place. She bowed her head, affording him full access. Instead of gratifying him, the sight of her bent in submission made him swallow hard. This wasn't right. This wasn't right for either of them.

He tugged her to her feet, making her stand to face him. Her gaze questioned him, unsure of what he wanted. Long practice made him want to sweep her off her feet and kiss her into full and unbridled certainty. He put a finger under her chin instead, tilting up her face.

"Meg, how long has it been since you've been held?"

"Held? What do you mean?"

"Like this." He hooked both of her arms around his neck. Careful where he placed his hands, he brought her to him, holding her loosely around the waist. "Everybody needs to be held, Meg. Even you."

She raised her head suspiciously, which confirmed his suspicion that she wasn't quite as sure of herself as he needed her to be. "What do you mean?"

"Try," he suggested.

Distrust stiffened her. Ready to retreat at the slightest provocation, she barely skimmed him with her length.

He chuckled to reassure her. "Don't worry, Meg. This isn't that kind of hug."

"It isn't?"

"No. We need a little more time, I think, before we end up in bed together."

"We do?"

"Don't you think so?"

"I suppose," she said doubtfully. Doubt he had previously gone out of his way to plant.

Tightening his hold, he placed his hands safely at the small of her back. She waited, standing still before she finally inched forward, exerting the barest hint of pressure against the ruffles of his shirt.

The simple drape of her dress swept the long line

of her spine and warmed his palms, luring him to picture what lay underneath. He concentrated on keeping his own hands steady and relatively flat, and realized how intricate the art of comfort and silence really was.

She moved to rest her head on his shoulder and held her breath as though listening. Maybe she was.

He thought of many things in that moment, thought of the corners of the room, the furniture, anything to make himself into a statue.

Sounds came through the walls of the hotel. Distant sounds. He recognized not a one, only that they were far away, and he and Meg were alone. Completely alone.

He controlled the natural response of his body, using it as an exercise in discipline, like he did with martial arts. She became like a sparrow to him, with his mission being to coax her, feed her even. He measured his success by what she entrusted him with.

Eventually she sighed. Hearing her relief, he focused on what it took to give her more. He cupped the back of her head, imagining Katie, of how he'd hold and comfort her.

Except he couldn't forget Meg was the one he held. She fit him, intimately, her woman's body shaped to meet his. All he had to do was lift her against him and the desire he had barely leashed would be exposed.

Yet he remained still. What he wanted and what she needed were two different things. Much as he might regret passing on the present opportunity, he had a wife to consider now, and they had to maintain some semblance of a relationship because of the child they shared.

Dropping his arms, Jack stepped back. She dropped her arms, too, folding them behind her back, studying him with a new yet grudging respect. "You don't know how much that helped me," she said.

"I'm glad," he replied, though the couch where he would spend the night mocked him.

"Well…" She retreated a step. "I guess this means good night."

"Good night."

She turned towards the bedroom in her ivory gown, gliding away from him like a current-drawn swan.

"Meg?"

"Yes?" She paused at the door.

"Don't let the bedbugs bite."

But Jack wished the bedbugs *were* biting a few days later, once he had officially settled in the suburban wilds of Oradell, New Jersey. Even bedbugs were preferable to dodging hordes of paparazzi by day and tossing and turning in a narrow twin bed by night. Jack had never felt so frustrated in his entire life.

Building Meg's trust would resolve his sexual frustration, but Katie was proving to be the real challenge. She accepted him into the household easily enough. He soon discovered, however, that the concreteness of life and death was a lot easier to explain to a four-year-old than what happened in the middle of the night when her eyes were closed.

She wasn't going to be denied this time, either.

Adamant, she stomped her pajama-clad foot. "I don't care what you say. They dance all night. I know they do. My bear and my bunny and my dollies dance, too."

Jack settled on the floor of her room with his back against the side of her frilly pink bed, and considered the pint-size shoe he held in his hands. The primary focus of their discussion, a pair of shiny black patent leather shoes, did not exactly lead to answers. The last couple of weeks with Katie had taught him how rarely the laws of physics applied to the imaginative world of a four-year-old girl.

He placed the shoes side by side and rubbed his jaw, giving Katie the benefit of his most serious deliberation. "I checked your shoes last night after you went to sleep, Katie. I never saw them move."

"But they don't start dancing till even grown-ups are asleep."

"How can you be absolutely, positively sure?"

She nodded emphatically, not even tempted by his show of skepticism. "I have an idea," he said.

Fifteen minutes later, he returned, armed with the Betz family video camera. Allen had not been the type to leave the important moments of life unrecorded. Jack also, very fortunately, believed every moment was important, from Katie's first hiccup as an infant to the girl Jack had come to know. After Katie went to bed, he would spend his evenings reviewing the backlog of the Betz family videotapes.

Now Jack zoomed in on the shelves of dolls, recording whether they were sitting, standing, the up-and-down position of arms. At his request, Katie ran to open her closet. The camera's viewfinder filled with stuffed animals. "Do you think all your toys come alive in the middle of the night?" he asked.

She nodded, firm in her belief. He scanned the lot of them, wondering if this idea had a chance in hell of working. Katie was a lot like her mother. They both possessed a belief system that bordered on pure stubbornness.

Once he finished cataloging everything in the room, he rewound the tape, then let Katie compare the images on the viewfinder to the objects in the room. "Tomorrow we'll check this tape again. You'll see for yourself that the toys haven't moved."

"But they *never* move," she declared.

Jack scratched his head in confusion. "I thought you said they danced all night."

"Don't you *know anything?* They always go back to their exact right places."

What a pistol she was.

She bustled with energy. Not J.J.'s energy, headlong and hell-bent, but the purposeful kind. She loved to set things in order.

She hosted elaborate tea parties between her stuffed toys and dolls. Dolls always got to drink first, and they had to have real water in their cups. Teddy bears did not.

Her favorite plush rabbit with pink satin ears got priority seating. Unfortunately, the designated throne for grown-ups changed without rhyme or reason, and pity the poor guy who didn't magically make the "tea" disappear when Katie's back was turned.

She made up stories based on her picture books, going into long soliloquies about what she saw on the pages. She was able to do it by herself, too, when he was forced to take a pressing call from his office the three days a week he got to spend with her, flying solo.

And talk. How she talked on and on about being a princess when she grew up. Or a firefighter.

"What about being a doctor or a nurse?" he asked.

She wrinkled her button nose and shook her dark head. Too many messes to clean up, she said. And doctors and nurses gave icky shots. Icky shots didn't save people. But princesses and firefighters did.

Jack wished he could tell Katie she was a princess—his princess. She had already saved someone. Him.

Eight

"**M**eg, I warned you this would happen. The paparazzi are insatiable."

To show how upset she was, she jerked the curtains over the living room windows, shutting out the morning light. "I told you so? Is that all you have to say?"

"We can't stay in this house," he said, repeating the same old refrain. "The cameras, the reporters are not going to go away."

The cut-and-dried statement sent her stalking to the kitchen. With Katie still asleep upstairs, the last thing Meg wanted to do was raise her voice, not to mention allow the parasites lurking around the house to find out that she and Jack were engaged in another one of their heated *discussions*. She banged the coffeemaker into production, taking refuge in the ritual.

"It's been weeks since we married. Surely they will leave us alone at some point."

"This problem is not going to solve itself. I don't know how to put it any plainer than that. We need to move—now."

Meg faced him. "How do you put up with the constant attention, Jack?" she asked in a choked voice. "I feel like a monkey in a cage."

"It's a fact of life."

"Not my life, it's not."

He folded his arms. "So you think you can pout and they'll all disappear?"

Meg, too, folded her arms. "Don't talk to me like a child."

Exasperated, he blew out a gust of air. "Why won't you consider moving to my apartment in New York? It's across the street from Central Park, it's close to your work, there are museums galore, and you and Katie won't be such oddities."

"Is that what Katie and I have become?" she bristled. "Oddities?"

"It comes with the territory. You're a Tarkenton now."

His name and his blood. Turning her back on him, Meg gripped her mug with both hands. He was right—she had to deal with the reality of the situation. But if they moved into Jack's swanky penthouse apartment, she'd be lucky to find another family in the building, much less one with children Katie's age.

Yet that building was completely safe.

The Tarkentons didn't talk about it much, but security considerations ruled them wherever they went. Their wealth and political influence made them targets for the crazies of the world. Meg knew for a fact that Bram and Amanda had discussed hiring a bodyguard for J.J., especially once he started school. Such precautions came with the territory, as Jack said.

Meg stared out the backyard window. Jack came to stand beside her. Such a small thing, too, to share a view, but it made her feel that perhaps there were some things they could face together.

"I know this house means a lot to you," he said. "If you want, we can put off selling for a while—there's no sense in alerting the world to our plans. The sales proceeds, of course, will go to you."

His talk of money left her feeling cold inside. Why didn't he understand? "I was six months pregnant when Allen and I bought this house," she murmured, still looking out the window. "The day Katie was born, he planted that tree that's in the backyard."

"A veritable saint, your Allen."

Something about the strain in Jack's tone made her turn around and consider him. "Is that the real reason you don't want to live here? Because Allen did?"

"No one can compete with a dead saint. I learned that when my father died. You want to hold on to Allen, fine. Just don't endanger our daughter in the process."

With the decision to move made, where to go remained the question. Meg rejected the city flat out, claiming she was looking for far more than safety or convenience. She wanted a place where the three of them could be a regular family.

The Tarkenton estate popped to Jack's mind. Meg immediately warmed to the idea, citing Katie's familiarity with the place. She would also have a chance to get to know Eleanor better, Meg added, though neither Eleanor nor Katie would ever know the true extent of their bond.

Jack made the arrangements, and by the end of March, they were ensconced in their own private wing of the mansion. To avoid gossip among the servants, he insisted that Meg share the master suite with him, but since it consisted of two separate bedrooms joined by a luxury bathroom, she didn't put up much of a fuss. He thought it a good sign for other reasons as well, but was reluctant to push the issue until he knew for certain that Meg had worked through her grief about Allen.

To allay any problems Katie might have with the transition, Jack had her new room painted the same color as her old one, and made sure he and Meg were with her when the movers came to pack her furniture. Katie watched the entire process with her thumb in her mouth, and screamed when the doors closed on the moving van.

But they were prepared for that. Meg sat in the back seat of the Jaguar with her as he followed the van to the estate. But it was still traumatic for her. The ghost of Allen still lived in the questions she asked. She wanted to know if he'd be able to see her from heaven if she lived somewhere else. How would he find her?

Meg answered as best she could. Jack put in his two cents' worth when necessary but found that the closer he got to the estate, the more resentful he grew. At least Allen's tree wouldn't be around anymore as a constant reminder of the man Katie and Meg had lost.

* * *

Jack saw the color of the gown first. Emerald green steeped in deep aqua blue, the rippling fabric shimmered down the length of Meg's body, though there wasn't a bead on it. It was more than a gown, he realized. It was a work of art.

His first thought was he wouldn't let her wear it. Erotic in the extreme, it flowed down the stairs as she did, innate with her fluidity and grace. Once she walked into the gala tonight, every man there would strip her in his mind and want that high-breasted, willowy body for his own.

Diamonds dripped from her hand. "Would you mind?" she asked, handing him the jewelry.

"Did Allen give you this?"

"I bought it myself, actually. You don't have to worry about how much it cost," she said. "It's fake."

She turned away from him and lifted her hair, releasing a wave of fragrance, the fragrance that still haunted his dreams. The clean pearlescence of her neck matched his memory of her breasts, emphasized by the clinging cut of her dress.

He tossed the rhinestones on the nearest table. "I won't have a wife of mine wearing cheap costume jewelry. Come on," he said, taking her hand and leading her down the main hall.

"Where are we going?"

"You'll see."

She came willingly enough, although the quick staccato of high heels on marble revealed how fast he was moving. He tucked her hand through the crook of his arm and, slowing his gait, spoke low. "Can you keep a secret?" he asked.

"Of course."

"Not even Katie can know."

Meg looked a bit taken aback by that. "What havoc are you about to unleash on me tonight?"

"Don't tempt me."

"Wait a minute—"

"We're here. Hush, now." Halting, he touched his finger to his lips and used his other hand to search the paneled wall behind him, feeling for the secret button disguised there. Suddenly the entire wall slid aside, revealing an open doorway. He pulled Meg in after him before the wall closed silently behind them, cutting off all light.

"Jack?" she gasped, grabbing his arm.

"Don't worry," he replied, addressing an electronic keyboard outlined in fluorescent green. He punched in the security code and another door automatically opened, switching on the recessed lighting that illuminated a large but entirely windowless room.

She glanced around like a curious bird, poised on the threshold of a whole new world.

Her fingers tensed, interlocking with his. "Don't worry," he repeated, and he led her inside. He'd designed the room to appear smaller than the twelve-by-twelve feet it actually was, making the walls close in with floor-to-ceiling black lacquer cabinetry and matching desk. Unadorned except for a leather writing pad and pen set, the desk and its companion chair were the only furnishings. Jack moved to stand behind them, regarding Meg with a hint of pride even though he couldn't tell her all that he did here. "How do you like my den?"

"Your den?" she echoed, glancing around, a hand

to her delectable but very naked throat. "Is that what this place is?"

"A den, an office, a vault, a bomb shelter."

"Bomb shelter?" She turned startled eyes on him.

"Sorry. Bad joke. The first three, yes. Last one, no."

"I was ready to believe you." Clasping her hands behind her back, she circled the room, flowing in and out of the incandescent beams spilling down from above, the vividness of her colors like a waterfall against the dark walls.

He watched her drift while he prowled. Wanting coursed through his veins. "Would you like a drink?" he asked.

"We'll be drinking at the gala."

"One for the road, then," he said, opening the large cabinet that revealed a fully equipped bar. He poured them both a Scotch on the rocks. "Let me show you why I brought you here," he said, handing over her glass.

"I'm almost afraid to ask," she admitted, sipping her drink.

The jewels were in the vault. He didn't want to overwhelm her, so he brought out only two cases. She was sensitive about the extent of his wealth, about living among his family's heirlooms.

Opening the cases, he presented the necklaces to her. Nestled on beds of black velvet, the emeralds reflected the awe in her eyes while the sapphires brought out their depths of blue.

"Oh, my," she whispered.

He would never forget the allure of that sound, her saying nothing, soft as air. He would never forget how she looked in that moment, either, vibrant and full of life.

"Go on, Meg," he urged. "Choose."

"I don't know if I can. I'll worry the whole time we're at the gala. What if I lost it? I'd never be able to forgive myself."

"Let me worry about that."

She tilted her head in indecision, nudging the bright jewels. "Which do you think looks best with this dress?"

He studied her deliberately long. "Hmm. Hard decision."

"If you don't make it soon we'll miss the opening of the gala," she observed dryly.

He set down the boxes and lifted the necklaces, one in each hand. Facing her, he draped one over each of her bared shoulders, using the action as an opportunity to brush her skin. Stepping back, he stroked his chin. "I don't know," he said thoughtfully.

Her wise eyes told him she didn't believe him for a minute. The rising color on her cheeks told him more. To see her so affected gave him the measure of control he needed to lift the emeralds and settle them around her neck. Holding the jeweled clasp closed in back, he put a thumb to the hollow of her throat, testing the fit. But what he was really testing was the rapidity of her pulse.

He hadn't experienced such a rush since he was a teenage boy, raging with hormones and awkward with need. Except now he knew exactly where to touch a woman, and exactly how.

He centered the necklace by feel alone, measuring the throb of her heart, the quickening heat of her

skin. He moved behind her for the best view possible, but she turned her head, keeping an eye on him.

"What are you doing?"

"Nothing." He fastened the necklace and stepped
back. There were parts of this game that required an
exquisite sense of timing. "How does it feel?"

"Why do you continue to do this to me?"

He loved innocuous questions. He loved playing
the game of cat and mouse, captor and captive, of
making conversation an art, rich with innuendo and
blame. He knew it was his turn to push, so he ambled
over to her, innocently asking the obvious question.
"Just what exactly am I doing to you?"

"Hurting me."

"Hurting you?" He kissed her gently on the lips
and pulled back, amused. "How could that hurt?"

"It hurts because it isn't real."

"Show me what's real, Meg."

She surprised him. She didn't hesitate. She kissed
his cheek and lingered, then looked at him. "A Judas
kiss. That's what it feels like to me."

She had the beauty of the converted, the charisma
of her faith. As though to prove it, she offered her
mouth again to him.

He took full advantage, intoxicated by the freedom
she gave him. The dress was like water in his hands,
unresisting and fluid to the touch. He shaped her
body with it, hearing the whisper of silk and what
the sound of it did to him.

She opened his coat, sliding her hands up his back
and stretching to meet him.

Warning bells went off in his mind. She was turning the tables, or attempting to, at least. He slowed

her down by nipping her tongue, her lips. "Is this what you want, Meg? Is this real?"

"I'm surrendering."

That pronouncement chilled his heart. He tried to push past it, push past her and make her be the one who drew the line.

He jerked her to him; she didn't protest. He pinned her to the wall, taking her breath, and realized how close he was to truly hurting her.

But it wasn't enough to get her to stop.

Her kiss found him, giving and beyond lush. He fought to eliminate the passion she brought to him, but he'd gone so long without. She tugged at his shirt, and her fingertips slid under the waistband of his trousers.

Desperate, he grabbed her up and swept aside the accessories on his desk, pulling her down on top of him.

It wasn't one of his wisest moves.

She was pliant, yet heavy enough to feel the way his body strained to fit hers. He couldn't hide his arousal. She made it infinitely worse, too, because she gave him her weight and opened her mouth to him.

For a moment, he joined her. He let her win.

It wasn't bad. It should be, though. It should be monumental in its clarity that if she surrendered to him totally, he would lose something precious. He couldn't name what it was, but the fear divided him completely, making him recall the one dream he hadn't been able to shake. He was his father's son, John B. Tarkenton Jr., and he had one heck of a reputation to uphold.

He lifted her up and switched places with her. She

wore hose, silken and erotic in the extreme. Sand-wiched by sensation, his hands rounded her hips, shedding the nylon.

She hiked a leg, and he hooked it around his hip, opening his trousers in the process. She pushed them down along with his briefs and clung to him, opening her mouth, and he plundered it the same way he plundered her body, feeling how good she was for him, how good she was to him.

It was the last thing he had envisioned, to take her like this, in this secret place, yet the fantasy of it gripped his imagination.

He wrapped her legs around his waist and drove into her. Rich sensation had him grasping for more. Cradling her back, he sought her mouth, her kiss, but the connection he wanted was elsewhere.

Glazed by passion, her gaze held his, entreating him with need. Control deserted him. Exploding within her, he became mindless of all but the beacon of her eyes, anchoring him to the awesomeness of complete and total pleasure. It had always been this way with Meg, and for once in his life, he didn't feel ashamed of losing his vaunted self-control.

Relaxing, he laid her gently down on the desk. It didn't take long to give her the same pleasure she gave him.

They ended up skipping the gala, and snuck past the servants to spend the rest of the night in the same bed. But Jack didn't sleep. Instead he watched peace steal over Meg's face.

Peace wasn't possible for him. Faith in the future was even harder to grasp. Days of faith were days gone by, days when he had been young and too full of himself—like now. But if having faith meant having a future with Meg, he had to give it another try.

Was this what love was supposed to feel like? He wasn't sure. And he needed to be absolutely sure before he said anything.

She knew he was sensitive about the subject of Allen. From Jack's point of view, Meg supposed he had reason to be jealous. What she didn't understand was why he kept bringing Allen's name into every conversation, especially when Jack had already told her he had no intention of trying to compete with the man.

She called Jack on it when they were dressing for a political fund-raising dinner one evening. He stood in front of the dressing room mirror, tying his four-in-hand tie, refusing to even consider the idea that after three months of life as a family, Katie had become quite fond of him. "Don't blow what Katie might think about me out of proportion," he said. "She's just a little girl."

"Your little girl."

He met her gaze in the mirror. "Yours, Meg."

"Doesn't it hurt that she doesn't know the truth?"

"I don't want her to know."

The crispness of his tone warned her not to pursue the subject, but Meg decided she couldn't let him get away with it this time. If they were ever going to get past his jealousy of Allen, Jack had to come clean about why he didn't want to acknowledge Katie in any way, shape or form.

"If Allen were in your position, he wouldn't be half as magnanimous."

"He doesn't have to be. He's dead."

"That's not what I meant at all. Why do you keep putting words in my mouth?" She presented him with her back. "Could you zip me up, please?"

He could and did, restraining himself from doing anything else. They were already running late.

"Don't you see what you're doing? Don't you see how your worship at the feet of Allen hurts Katie?"

"He was a man, Meg. No better or worse than most. It's not a crime for a man to lust after a woman, especially when he's smart enough to make that woman his wife."

"He was trying to help me."

"Justify it any way that you want. You want to make him the good guy and me the bad guy, go ahead. Join the line. It forms on the left."

"Don't get smart with me."

"Allen was the smart one. He married you first. He was the best husband a wife could have. You don't have to tell me. I already know. I'll never be his equal. Thank you. I'll keep it in mind."

She stared at him. "That's the story of your life, isn't it? You'll never measure up no matter how hard you try."

He held her gaze just to show her he could, knowing exactly how to avoid her stab in the dark. "Come here," he said.

She bit that lush lower lip of hers, the one he planned to ravish the moment she came near.

"Will you meet me halfway?" she asked.

He came within an arm's length of her, but she didn't move.

She spoke instead. "No one should have to lose a father the way you lost yours, Jack, in such a brutal fashion."

He shrugged. "It wasn't so brutal. The clips on TV showed it from every possible angle known to man. The bullets went right through him. He didn't feel a thing."

Knowing how callous he sounded, he waited for her to touch him, to offer comfort. The moment she did, he would push her down on the bed and finally take her.

She bent low as though to put on a pair of shoes. That was odd. He felt her lay her cheek upon his hand and he felt the faintest stirring of sorrow. He couldn't imagine why. Fortunately, he didn't give in to it.

She did. She wept against his hand. He couldn't push her down and make love to her when she was crying. He sifted through her hair instead, waiting until she stopped and the danger passed.

She lifted her head and finally looked at him, putting the back of her hand against his cheek. That was his clearest signal yet. She wanted to be gathered and taken to bed. The wonder of her body would make him forget the problems in his life.

He could make her forget her problems, too. He would get her heart to pounding and her skin to heat, and then he'd delve deep. When the moment of satisfaction came, he would be filled with the certainty that he was alive. It would hold him for a while. Hold him until he needed her again.

And he felt how much he needed her now.

Except he couldn't bring himself to touch her. All he had to do was push her down and she would open her body to him. But he couldn't bring himself to do it. It was the strangest sensation.

Her eyes filled again with tears. He didn't understand why she cried, why she withdrew and left the room, closing the door softly in her wake.

He sat by himself and studied the foreign look of his tears, warm and wet on the palms of his hands.

Nine

The moment he drove through the gates of the estate, Jack sensed something was different. Tom, the security guard, gave the usual thumbs-up sign. The thumbs-up was normal. The usually taciturn man's grin was not.

Jack parked in the garage, noting that his mother's Bentley was absent. That was unusual. She made a great deal of the dinner hour, especially with a family to preside over.

He didn't suspect Meg was behind it all until he spotted her lounging at the doorway of the house, barefoot in leggings and a leopard-print sweater, the most raucous smile on her face.

"You want champagne, mister?"

She raised the uncorked bottle in her hand, but before he found the breath to answer, she drank from it herself, straight up.

"Where is everybody?"

"Gone."

With a pirouette, she was gone herself. Loosening his tie, he followed his nose into the kitchen which, though empty of staff, smelled delicious nonetheless. "Meg?"

"Here." She paused in the hall like the sprite she was.

"What about my mother and Katie?"

"Your mother was kind enough to take Katie away for the night. I told everyone I was getting an awful cold and *vanted to be alone*," she said in dramatic fashion.

"Alone?"

"With my husband to take care of me, of course. Champagne, anyone?"

She lifted the bottle of champagne to her lips and, eyeing him boldly, guzzled straight from the bottle. Or tried guzzling, at any rate. Guzzling wasn't part of Meg's repertoire. Yet the effort she put into it impressed him no end.

"Meg, you know the rules. Spill any of that champagne and we'll both be in trouble."

"I thought you liked trouble." She offered the bottle, mischief in her eyes. "Come and get it."

"Oh, no, you don't. You come to me."

"That gets boring after a while, don't you think?"

She hid the bottle behind her back, retreating like the feline she was, placing each foot sideways with stealthful care. Seeing the way she moved affected him strongly, and he felt how much he wanted to keep her safe, even from something as undangerous as the furniture in the room. "You better watch where you're going," he warned.

She nodded and smiled and brought the bottle to her mouth, crinkling her nose at him. She drank.

How he wanted to capture that moment, capture her and keep her forever. He leaped for her, but she sprang into the dining room, putting the mahogany table between them.

He chuckled because he couldn't help it. Damn, she was quick. And funny and brilliant and more and more beautiful every day.

Matching her show of stealth, he kicked off his shoes and socks, then took on the aura of a predator, ready to spring. He circled the table and she did the same, keeping them on opposite sides. "You know you can't escape," he told her.

"Wanna bet?"

He chuckled at her slang and jumped. The suddenness of his move had her shrieking with laughter. He cornered her and put his arms up, capturing her there.

She knew it was over, knew she was caught. She didn't try to hide the bottle. She closed off the top and shook it instead.

He caught her hands but wasn't able to elude the frothy explosion when she let go. It doused him. Doused her, too. That's when he took the bottle away.

"I do love champagne," he admitted. "Especially on you."

He tipped the bottle upside down over her head. She tilted up her chin and opened her mouth, swallowing down the last few drops, the long column of her throat exposed to him. He kissed that throat, sipping champagne until he hit the cleavage of her breasts.

He wanted her naked. He wanted her now.

Her fingers were busy with the buttons of his shirt. He ripped it off, popping buttons, and she had the temerity to giggle.

"What are you laughing at?"

"It's not what I'm laughing at, but whom. You, my dear husband, you."

He kissed her for the sudden sting he felt behind his eyes, kissed her for saying what he needed to hear, and for making it possible for him to not say anything at all.

He leaned into her. It was the wall that held them up, the wall and the urgency of desire. They always had the desire. Except now it was fueled by his sense that he had time to see and hear and touch her all over. It was allowed.

He saw how she divined what he felt. Her gaze grew tender and she laid her hand alongside his face.

He copied the gesture, feeling the firmness of her cheek and the generosity that lay beneath it. He snagged the wet tangles of her hair, moved beyond words, and kissed her with gentleness, even though need hurried him. He wanted better than "hurried". He wanted the best for her, wanted it to be the best for them. "Tell me what you want," he whispered. "Tell me what you like best."

She whispered in his ear. He did exactly as she said. In the end she wanted to be carried to their bed. That sneaking suspicion he had from the beginning was right on.

He didn't know what else to do with the enormity of his feeling. He could only show her in this way and hope it was enough.

* * *

"Daddy?"

"Yes, Katie," Jack answered, intent on the newspaper he held open before him. Then he froze. Had she truly said—

"Daddy, are you listening to me?" she demanded.

"Of course," he answered as the headlines in front of him wavered. But he couldn't put the paper down to check those big brown eyes of hers. Katie might see how shaken he was. "Can we go to the zoo?" she asked.

"The zoo?" he echoed, hiding behind his paper. "Now?"

She giggled. "Of course not, silly. It's morning."

As usual, the way her mind worked caught him flat-footed. "Isn't the zoo open in the morning?"

"Yes. But we can't go today."

"We can't?"

"It's Sunday, silly."

"Sunday." He lowered the paper and her eyes twinkled at him. This was one of her favorite games. "Are you sure?"

"Sure I'm sure. I have my pj's on."

"Don't you usually wear your pj's on Sunday?"

"Of course, silly."

Meg entered with a fresh stack of pancakes. "Katie knows that today is Sunday because her pajamas are on. Every other day of the week, she'd have her clothes on by now."

He sensed Meg hadn't heard what started this conversation. He didn't want her to, either. He was shaken enough as it was.

"Mommy, do we have to go to church today?" Katie asked.

"Yes, punkin'."

"I want Daddy to come, too."

The *D*-word arrested Meg the same way it had arrested him. Her fork stopped midway between the stack of pancakes and Katie's plate, but the moment passed in an instant. "Jack's not your daddy, sweetheart," Meg said, moving smoothly on to stack pancakes on her own plate.

Her cool words stole his joy. Except he didn't know if it was joy or some other foreign emotion. But Katie was oblivious to everything but her need to be heard. "I want Jack to be my daddy now."

She slipped off her chair and crawled into his lap, wreathing his neck, and the magic of what she called him returned. And the worst part was, he wanted to look at Meg and share it with her. He couldn't, though. It was far too big a risk.

He didn't go to bed with her that night. For the first time in months, he sat alone in his den until well after midnight, drinking straight malt whiskey, noticing little but the burn in his mouth, down his throat, behind his eyes.

My God. He was a father now.

The moment Katie called him Daddy, Meg spoke the lie and heard the lie and knew the lie for what it was. A shield. But like any weapon taken in battle, it was difficult to put down.

Jack didn't make it any easier. He withdrew from her. He withdrew from everyone. Even Katie noticed it. That's when Meg knew she had to do something. She had to take matters into her own hands.

She discussed his distance with Amanda one day. She listened for a long time and gave good advice, that Meg had to keep the faith and wait for him to come to her, but that wasn't what her gut instinct said.

Even with Katie, his mind was far away.

And his body never betrayed him, which made Meg anxious inside. Sure, she missed the sex. But she missed the small intimacies they used to share more. She missed their being husband and wife, to have and to hold, for better or worse, richer or poorer, in sickness and in health, as long as they both shall live.

And that was the point. They weren't together anymore. Jack made it official when he moved back to the other bedroom.

And for the first time Meg saw how the lie might have hurt him. It hurt Katie, too. Every time she called him Daddy, she spoke the truth without knowing it.

Such a small piece of knowledge it was, too. Just a matter of timing and organisms so microscopic, they couldn't be seen. Except in the color of Katie's eyes. And it was becoming harder and harder for Meg to look into those eyes. The lie had become that big.

She saw how it affected Eleanor, too. How she loved to sit and comment that J.J. reminded her of his grandfather. The grandfather he and Katie shared.

Meg definitely felt the most guilt with Eleanor.

The revelation didn't come all in one moment. But there came a time when the cost of perpetrating such a fundamental lie outweighed the benefit of keeping silent. Now when Meg thought of her family, she considered the concept of what family really meant, of what it was really for. And the family that came first in her heart was the one she had made with Jack.

The distant murmur of Meg's voice reached Jack when he was halfway up the stairs. He'd come to move out the rest of his clothes and immediately halted, not wanting to disturb her. By the sound of it, she was reading Katie a story.

Her bedroom door must be wide open. Now that he had stopped moving, he heard Meg's voice clearly, heard the turning of the pages. The book was by Dr. Seuss. The story featured Horton the elephant. Helped by the rhyming rhythm of the words, Katie was reading it herself, going on for sentences at a time. Pride swelled him. He could see them in his mind's eye, sitting in the rocker together, Katie holding her rabbit, underlining every word with her finger.

She rarely sucked her thumb anymore. She'd really grown up in the last year.

He heard them finish the end together, heard the closing of the book and Meg's murmur that it was time to go to sleep.

"Mommy, do you love Daddy?" Katie asked.

He gripped the banister, knowing he should retreat. This was a private conversation. But when Meg answered, he couldn't move.

"Yes, I do, sweetheart. I love Daddy very much."

"Is that why you married him?"

"That's one reason. Jack loves you, too. That's another reason."

"He sure gives me lots of presents."

"It's hard for him to say how much he loves you. So he gives you presents instead."

"Does he give you presents?"

"Yes, he does."

"Like what?"

"Well, he gave me this ring. It means he loved me enough to marry me."

"Will he give me a ring someday?"

"Not a wedding ring. That's for when people get married. But maybe another kind of ring, as a present, when you're older."

"How old do you have to be?"

"Not any age in particular."

"How old to get a wedding?"

Meg laughed, the sound tinkling softly like ice in a glass. "How old do you think, Katie?"

"Old enough to have a baby?"

"Older than that. Taking care of a baby is a big job for anybody. It's important to finish school. It's important to have a job. It's important to get married before the baby comes, too, because both the mommy and the daddy have to work together and help each other take care of it."

"Is that what you and my first daddy did?"

"Yes, Katie. We did our best to help each other."

"Do you miss him?"

"Yes."

"Me, too. I want to go see him in the place he died."

"You mean the cemetery?"

"Uh-huh. I want to put some flowers there."

"All right. We'll make it a point to stop there tomorrow."

"Will my new daddy come with us?"

"I don't know. You'll have to ask him."

"He doesn't like my first daddy, does he?"

"I don't know about that, Katie. He never met your first daddy."

"Who do you like better?"

"Of your two daddies? Oh, Katie, I can't choose like that."

"Why not?"

"I love them both. What about you? Can you choose between them?"

"I like my first daddy best."

"Why?"

"He loved me best."

"Even though he didn't give you lots of presents?"

"He told me he loved me. And he answered all my questions, Mommy."

"Your new daddy doesn't do that?"

She must have started crying then, for Meg made a soothing sound and he heard Katie sob.

Backing down the stairs, Jack went out of the house. He stood in the front for a while, noticing the flowers that bloomed there. Flowers Katie and Meg had planted.

He walked around and saw more. Both of them loved flowers.

He went inside and picked up the phone and dialed a number he used often when he was a swinging single. This time he ordered three big bouquets. One for Meg, one for his mother and one for Katie to lay on Allen's grave.

Then he returned upstairs, making some noise so Meg would know it was him. Katie's door was ajar. He looked in. She was asleep.

He heard the shower running and wandered down the hall to the bedroom he used to share with Meg.

The door was open, but the door to the bathroom was closed. He turned the knob, but it was locked.

He thought about picking the lock. He thought about Meg standing naked in the shower, and how he wanted to stand under the spray with her and make himself clean.

If only he could.

Ten

Meg had the look of a girl today. Though the temperature was chilly for late May, she wore a sleeveless lemon yellow dress that matched the brilliance of the sun. Surprised to see her playing with Katie in full view of the usual throng of paparazzi camped at the gate, Jack went to investigate.

Meg had to be up to something. It wasn't like her to expose Katie to the public eye. But she and Katie appeared not to have a care in the world.

An old-fashioned wooden swing hung from the biggest branch of one of the majestic old oaks that lined the drive. Seating Katie on the swing, Meg gave her a push. Katie squealed in delight, making Meg laugh. God, how he missed that sound.

Meg saw him and greeted him with a lively wave as though she was actually glad to see him. "I wondered where you were."

He nodded toward the snapping lenses. "Where else would I be with the morality police at our door?"

"I was thinking about having a little talk with them."

"What about?"

"Us."

She was smiling, which eliminated any topic related to "us" he could think of, and he told her as much.

"I don't know about that, Jack." She dropped to the ground and leaned back on her arms, squinting up at him. "I happen to think it's time the world knew who Katie's biological father really is."

Nonreaction was a useful skill in moments such as these, moments where he felt like his heart would beat right through his chest. Checking to make sure Katie was well out of earshot, he stood over Meg, his expression calm, his tone conversational. "When were you planning this little confession fest?"

"Katie should be told first, don't you think? Then our families, and finally, the public."

"How nice of you to think of Katie first." His voice dripped with sarcasm.

"I'd like you to be there with me. I may need help getting the story out. I'll certainly need your moral support."

Moral? Him? He snorted in disbelief. "If you think I'm going to support you on this, you're crazy."

"Tarkenton Goes to the Loony Bin. How's that for a headline?"

"Are you trying to get a rise out of me in front of our friends at the gate? Because it's not going to happen."

"No, Jack. I'm perfectly serious."

Unbelievably, she looked perfectly serious, too. "I won't let you do this."

"I don't want to lie anymore."

"It's not a lie. We're simply holding something back, something that is no one's business but our own."

"I happen to disagree."

"What about your mother, your sister and brothers? Don't you see what this will do to them, how this will hurt them and you?"

"They'll forgive me."

There was that gravity again, that complete and utter belief that everything would turn out fine. "Forget your family, then," he retorted. "What about mine? My mother will kill me for keeping this from her. If Amanda doesn't do the same, Bram certainly will. Is that why you're doing this? Because if you're trying to use Katie to get back at me, you will know hell, and I'll be the one to send you there."

"You're completely against it. I get the message."

"No, I don't think you do. I want to hear you swear on all you hold dear that you will keep your mouth shut."

"I'm sorry, Jack, but I can't do that. I have to do what I think is right."

"You'll destroy Katie."

"You know that isn't true."

"Look, Meg, you want to crucify me for being a jerk, fine. You have the right. I'm an adult. I can take it. Katie can't."

"She's not a baby, Jack. She needs to know the truth."

"What truth? That you and I screwed our brains out one weekend and she was the result?"

"I would never put it that crudely."

"No matter how many pretty ribbons you tied around it, there is only one conclusion that she will reach. She wasn't planned. She wasn't wanted. The tabloids will never let her forget it, either. Why would you want to hurt her like that? Why would you want her to know—" He broke off, sickened by the realization that Katie *would know* what he did. He had abandoned her deliberately, for years.

"The secret will come out sometime, Jack. Secrets like these always do. Our families deserve to hear it from us first."

"After what we've told them, do you actually think they are going to believe that five years ago you had an affair with me?"

"They'll believe me if you back me up. Will you?"

It was a simple-enough question. The undercurrents, however, ran deep. Meg didn't seem to realize that if she told the truth, what little peace they had found would be destroyed. "Is this some kind of test?" he demanded. "It is, isn't it? You want me to stand up and say I seduced you."

She drew back, astonished. "Is that really what you think—*you* seduced *me?*"

"What's your version of events?"

"I decided that if I was going to lose my virginity, I wanted to do it with someone experienced. My goodness, Jack, I was doing my darnedest to seduce you. I will admit, I was a little drunk—"

"Meg, you were plastered."

"I was not," she refuted with great dignity. "I had two glasses of wine. After dinner you and I went for a walk. We kissed. By that time, I knew exactly what I was after. I remember you drank quite a lot, though.'' She dimpled. ''It must have been before that famous story about you and the Betty Ford Clinic hit the stands.''

''I can't believe you're bringing up some asinine story in some asinine news rag. I barely got you into the hotel room before I attacked you.''

''We attacked each other. That's how I remember it.''

''Then your memory is damned faulty. I used you, Meg. And don't expect me to sit by while you tell our families about it, either. I'll file for divorce if I have to.''

''I have to tell the truth, Jack, with your support or without it.''

''What kind of mother are you?''

He scored a direct hit on that one. She lifted her chin. ''A good one.''

''I knew you were self-righteous, but what you're talking about is downright sick. Insane. And I will go that far if I have to, Meg. I'll have you declared mentally incompetent. I'll have you put away. You'll never see Katie again.''

''Losing a mother is a terrible thing for a child to endure,'' she replied. ''It might even rank right up there with losing a father.''

''Don't bring my father into this, dammit. This is about you and me, Meg. It's always been about you and me. It's enough that we know the truth. Don't let it hurt Katie. Don't let the stink of it mess up her life. Once the tabloids get wind of it, they will make how she was conceived seem sordid and wrong. Allen is the one who deserves to be her father.''

''Katie has no reason to feel ashamed. She had no control over how she was conceived. It's you and I who carry the responsibility for the circumstances of her birth. Maybe it's hard for you to believe, but I thank God every day for how we came together, Jack. Sure I'm not proud of lying to my family about it. But there is no doubt in my mind that Katie was meant to be, that she came from something good, something you and I found in each other. Maybe it's not enough to sustain our marriage over the long term. But I'm not going to pretend it doesn't exist."

She claimed to care what he thought, but she wasn't listening to a word he said. He wanted to strangle her. He jammed his hands in his pockets instead. "You want to do this? Fine. But you have to tell your own family first."

"Will you be there with me?"

"I'll be there," he said, grating out the words. "But I won't be with you. I'm not going to let you drop this little bomb on people and walk away clean."

She visibly paled. Good, he thought. He hoped he'd put the fear of God in her. He hoped she'd thought long and hard about what she was contemplating, and came to her senses very soon. He didn't want to think about what he would do if she didn't. The last thing Katie needed was to think he hadn't wanted her. He hadn't cared enough to come forward in the beginning.

"It's going to take some time to get everyone together," she said.

Hallelujah, he wanted to say. He headed for Katie and gave her a big push instead.

Even when Meg made the phone calls to gather her family together and flew her mother into JFK, Jack truly believed that in the end, her courage would falter. She'd never go through with her plan.

The reason why she was going to such lengths was because she needed proof of his undying love and affection.

The day before the official gathering, Meg informed him that not everyone could make it. Zach, her youngest brother, and his wife, Sarah, were overwhelmed with the late-spring demands of their Wyoming ranch. Meg's middle brother, Joe, was off in the wilds of Alaska somewhere, and her sister, Elizabeth, had already used up her vacation time coming out for all the events that had taken place the past year.

That pared the numbers from the Masterson clan down to two: Meg's mother and Bram. Unfortunately, Amanda showed up on her husband's broad arm, insisting she was a Masterson, too. And of course she was. Amanda had appointed herself to keep track of any and all family happenings on both sides of her family.

But Jack was surprised by the arrival of his mother.

It turned out Mary Masterson had mentioned it to her, apparently misunderstanding that the invitation had been extended only to her side of the family.

Ready to call a halt to the proceedings, Jack saw how the sight of his mother made Meg nervous as well. It then occurred to him the august presence of the one-and-only Eleanor Tarkenton might very well work to his advantage.

These four people were the core of their combined families, the ones Meg loved and respected the most.

They trooped down the hall and into the library. He'd insisted upon this room rather than one near the west wing where Katie was safely asleep. They gathered around the coffee table that centered a grouping of sofas and chairs.

Bram held a bottle of beer. The women balanced teacups on their knees, courtesy of the bone china tea set Meg had laid out herself. Why women dragged out the china in times of crisis, he didn't understand, but he figured such a civilized atmosphere promoted civilized discourse. He was there to guarantee it.

He experienced a mild sense of shock when Meg first used the word *sex*.

More than shock hit him when Meg confessed to deliberately wanting to seduce *him*. She then supplied enough details to establish just where and when the affair had taken place, making it graphically clear that Katie was conceived at Bram and Amanda's wedding. Allen Betz was not Katie's father. Jack Tarkenton was. Meg said it that way, too, as if he wasn't sitting right there beside her.

Amanda paled and looked straight at him, her mouth grim. His mother stared down at her tea.

Jack had ignored such looks before. He ignored them now. But when Bram reached to take Meg's trembling hands, Jack put a possessive arm around her. For she was still talking. And she was telling the truth about everything.

Except she was trying to make light of it, trying to lessen the look of disbelief that crossed her mother's face when she explained that the affair went on over the entire weekend.

No one at the table congratulated her, however. It didn't look like they were particularly proud, either, especially when she confessed that she hadn't been responsible about birth control, and Katie was conceived.

That's when Meg broke down. She wept and told them how sorry she was for lying to them. She hadn't wanted to burden them with her problems. That's why she married Allen. She didn't feel she could go to any of the Tarkentons because she was afraid if the news got out, Katie would forever be branded illegitimate.

Jack flinched at the word. *Illegitimate.* It wasn't possible for him to have an illegitimate child. In his world, there were no accidents. He didn't believe in twists of fate. When it came to birth control, he was entirely and utterly responsible. He had to be. Women of all ages had thrown themselves at him since adolescence. As the famous son of an infamous man, he'd been a target for social and political climbers all his life.

He'd always taken precautions. He practiced safe sex with the fervor of the religious. But for some inexplicable reason, he hadn't practiced it with Meg.

How many days had he paced his New York City apartment when he returned from the wedding, arguing with himself? So what if he was careless? So what if she stayed on his mind? It didn't matter that he promised to call her, not when she was gullible enough to take him at his word. He wasn't about to break his most cardinal of rules. The last thing he wanted was to get involved with anyone, especially a woman like her.

She didn't meet his usual standards. The rule was that he only slept with women with equal or greater sexual experience. Older women were best. They knew the score.

Meg had the smarts and sophistication of an older woman, but it was her education in France that gave her that polish. If he had any idea of the full extent of her innocence, he never would have gotten within ten feet of her. He certainly never intended for Meg to get pregnant. Such a concept didn't make sense. Ever since he'd reached adulthood, he'd made a career of shattering any and all expectations that might be required of him.

Meg wasn't different. He didn't love her. He didn't love anyone except Katie. Meg was merely the mother of his child.

He respected her, sure. So many fawned over him, trying to use him to get what they wanted. She didn't. He thought as much when he overheard her pronounce the name of an excellent but obscure wine with a perfect French accent. He knew it for certain when he saw how she stood out from the ordinary, from the crowd. She and her big brother Bram were the only members of the Masterson clan who didn't look bowled over by the presence of his family in all their reflected Tarkenton glory.

Jack recalled how close he'd come to skipping the rehearsal dinner. Already bored by the prospect of wasting an entire weekend on his sister's wedding, he arrived late, planning to leave as soon as the meal was served.

But his plans went out the window the moment he got together with Meg. She made the event memorable all by herself, simply by virtue of her presence. Alive with style, she glowed, and he told himself her fresh-faced look of the ingenue was a trick of the light.

The last morning they spent together, she wrote down her telephone number so he wouldn't forget. He hadn't, either. Even though he threw the paper away the moment she left, he could not erase the numbers from his mind.

So they shared the same city. With seven million other souls, odds were she'd never find him. He guarded his private domain like nowhere else. Servants and assistants insulated him from all comers, including his family. His secretary was the only one who knew how to reach him at a moment's notice.

Yet he walked around a phone he refused to pick up, even when it rang. After a week of driving himself crazy, he rerecorded the answering machine tape to say he was out of the country. Before leaving town, however, there were arrangements to be made. To ensure the recovery of his sanity, Jack visited the office of a certain private detective and paid a lot of money for the man to take a lot of pictures. Jack also left his forwarding address.

He wanted photos of Meg with other men. He said he would double the P.I.'s fee for a shot of her in bed with another man. That was one photo Jack knew he'd keep, even if he had to carry the damn picture in his wallet for the rest of his days. Never again would he make such a fool of himself.

A few days later, the P.I. sent him a list of all the men Meg supposedly had come in contact with since she had first moved to New York. Most Meg worked with. The rest owned the shops she frequented—the corner grocery, a French-style bakery and the discounters on Fifty-second Street.

Jack was living it up in Rio de Janeiro then, spending a lot of money to keep busy all the time. Or trying to.

The photos found him a week later, at the casinos of Monaco. There were candid shots of each of the men, but the P.I. reported Meg did not have a personal interest in any of them.

Jack burned the lot while toasting his great good sense in leaving New York City when he did.

He was cruising the Mediterranean when he got the news that Meg had quit her job as assistant curator of textiles at the Metropolitan Museum of Art. Even though she now earned a much higher salary, providing the latest-and-greatest fabrics to New York fashion designers, the fact that she had quit what she termed her dream job nagged at him.

He diverted himself with a quick trip to the Pyrenees, then decided to take on a real challenge and flew to the Himalayas for a trek up Everest. But the weeks of diversion exacted their toll, especially where Meg Masterson was concerned.

Check that. Meg Masterson Betz.

The news of her marriage reached him in Hong Kong. The first photo of the happy couple came by fax. Though the picture was blurred, there was no mistaking her outline, arm and arm with a pudgy man.

When the courier arrived with a series of eight-by-ten glossies, Jack couldn't believe his eyes. Allen Betz didn't seem Meg's type at all. Balding, overweight and bespectacled, her chosen one was a tax accountant who had just flunked his second CPA exam. According to the private investigator, he had long been a friend of the Masterson family, although Meg, because of her time at the Sorbonne, hadn't seen him in years.

The significance of the link struck Jack immediately. Ever since he had reached voting age, he'd deliberately pushed his family's well-meaning friends away. They knew how to lay on the guilt, constantly reminding him of the principles his father had lived by and died for, encouraging him to fight the good fight, to run for office and make a difference in the world. They failed to understand that there was only one John B. Tarkenton. And he had died a long time ago.

The investigator didn't ask why he was suddenly told to stop taking pictures. Jack did give him one last assignment, however, and it cost the most.

Paternity tests weren't that expensive. Keeping them secret was. The biggest chunk of change went to the hospital nurse who drew a tiny bit of the baby's blood when Meg delivered a seven pound, two ounce girl. Then a lab technician in another hospital was paid to type and test the blood against an unlabeled sample.

No one except the P.I. knew whose sample it was. And Jack paid an obscene amount to ensure that the nurse "forgot" the name of the baby she'd drawn blood from.

The convoluted nature of the scheme confused even him. At least, Jack felt confused when he saw the results. Or maybe it was simply the shock of discovering that he was a father.

He traveled from Hong Kong to Singapore to Bangkok, intent on forgetting in the pleasure capitals of the world. But instead of losing himself in his quest for the ultimate high, he found himself noticing faces. Especially those of the children. Children who lived, literally, on the streets.

Out of guilt he reached for his wallet. He gave out small bills, American, to small hands. The money would do some good that way. Dollars greased the black market. That's where the most nutritious food was.

Then Jack saw what the kids spent those dollars

on. Rather than support the local neighborhood drug lords, he bought the damned food from the black marketeers and doled it out himself. What started with a handful of kids swelled to hundreds in the space of one week.

He needed help. He didn't want to be seen this way, acting like he cared. If he cared, he would have stayed in New York.

Jack went to the religious charities that already had a presence in Thailand. He would provide the money if they would provide the work, the food, the care.

He got past the red tape of the local and national government with judicial use of the Tarkenton name. He had one condition, however. If he was ever identified as the benefactor, the funds would immediately dry up.

It took months to make the first shelter happen. The grand opening occurred a year to the day Katie was born.

Jack watched the ribbon-cutting from a dingy room in a dingy hotel across the street from the shelter. Even in the backwaters of Bangkok, he didn't want to risk being seen anywhere near such a venture.

A newborn baby happened to be abandoned that day, a tiny, half-starved girl. He witnessed people digging in excited consternation through a mound of garbage off the street and knew something was up. But when he saw the nun run outside and gather what was found to her chest, horror overwhelmed him. The baby didn't even have swaddling clothes.

He made one phone call. The next day her picture was in the newspaper alongside an article about the opening of the clinic and orphanage. Among the foreign characters of the Thai alphabet, Jack made out the initials of her name in the caption underneath.

K. T. Oolong was five years old now. Along with her many sisters and brothers, she had a drawerful of clothes and was enrolled in a school that the religious order ran in the newly renovated building next door to the shelter.

Of all the hundreds of children, K.T. was the only one he kept tabs on. In his wallet, he carried her picture. He made it a regular practice to study it as a tangible reminder of how close he'd come to losing what little conscience he had left.

A little girl's dark eyes smiled under her fringe of straight black hair. Never met, she was a dream to him, like getting to know his own daughter had once been a dream. Now he held on to the photo for no other reason than to commemorate his father. John B. Tarkenton once said his life's ambition was to make the world safe for the children.

That was why, despite his exercise training and sharp reflexes, he was lost in remembrance. Jerked to his feet, the punch to his gut caught Jack totally unawares.

"I figured I had a free shot for defiling my sister, you bastard. Now it's your turn." Bram Masterson grabbed him by the front of his shirt, holding him up.

Amanda quickly stepped between them. "Bram, this is not going to happen. You and Jack are not going to fight."

Bram showed disgust. "Amanda, he might be your brother but he's scum of the earth to me. This has been coming for a long time. We all know it. Take Meg and Mom and your mother and wait in the other room."

"I will do no such thing. Look at what you're doing to Meg. And dare I mention, Katie? She's got the biggest stake in this. All of us here are her family, the Tarkentons and the Mastersons both. We're all she's got."

Jack knew, as usual, his big sister was right on the mark. But some devil inside kept pushing him. "Come on, Masterson," he taunted Bram. "Take your shot."

It took the four women to keep them apart. Seeing the distress on Meg's face, Jack finally recognized the force that was forever pushing him, egging him on, always spoiling for a fight. "It wasn't defilement," he said to Bram and dropped his fists. "I loved her. I always did."

Seeing the stunned look on Meg's face, Jack felt the stranglehold of emotion, the fear of saying what could not be taken back. Maybe he shouldn't have admitted it. Certainly he didn't want to hurt her anymore.

The responsibility he suddenly felt tore at him. What if he failed miserably? Was it possible that John B. Tarkenton's son truly had the ability to step in the shoes of his father and claim the same dreams for himself?

Eleven

"**O**bviously, I think it is necessary."

"Why? Jack demanded, careful to keep his voice down. He and Meg were not alone. Katie was playing on her swing and the usual cadre of media types were hanging around the gates of the estate, telephoto lenses in their greasy little hands. He gestured towards them. "Why would you want to go anywhere near those goons? What could you possibly hope to get out of it?"

"I hate this feeling of being like a specimen under a microscope. It's time to identify the specimen. It's time to expose it to the air."

"You're not going to like how it smells."

"How do you know?"

"I know."

"Funny how I always felt I should believe you, even when I told myself I shouldn't."

"Well I'm glad part of you has some sense. What do I have to do to bring the rest around—charge the media for this peep show?"

She kissed him. He didn't allow it to go on for long. "You see the size of those photo lenses? Tonight those guys will be tendering million dollar offers."

"I don't care. I made promises to you, Jack. I want to honor them."

"You have honored your promises, Meg. Every last one. I haven't. It's that simple."

"You want to see simple? Watch this."

She walked toward the circus of media hanging around the gate. Katie ran after her, and that's when he ran, too, scooping Katie into his arms. For the first time in his adult life, Jack did not know what to do.

He had to protect Katie. He had to shut Meg up. But he couldn't stop her. One armed and determined individual could pretty much take anybody out. His father's assassination proved that.

Watching Meg step into the glaring light of publicity was like watching the last film that existed of his father, heading like a lamb to slaughter.

He glanced at Katie. He'd do anything to spare her the pain of seeing herself framed forever on TV for the entire world to see, stoic and silent in grief. Doggedly, he followed Meg, calculating what to do and say. "Hello," he began when he reached her side, addressing them all.

The reporters and cameramen helloed back, made friendly by this unprecedented and unsolicited approach.

Meg gave him a smile, but it was a nervous one.

He'd put the fear of God in her, that was plain. "My wife tells me that it's time to introduce our daughter to you. Katie, can you say hello to these people?"

Katie emphatically shook her head. A couple of the more human among the paparazzi laughed. Jack targeted them with his smile. "She's a little shy. She has only just turned five."

"Is she really your biological daughter?"

He shared a long and meaningful look with Meg. "She is."

It felt oddly like a movie to him, the parts scripted and assigned. At one point Katie ran back to the swing to play. He took Meg's hand. As always, her grace under fire was impressive.

Where did she find her deep well of faith? It carried her as it carried him. Yet she was so damned good at making herself look human, in spite of her inimitable style. Maybe that was why he found himself making jokes about how human he was, too.

"How long did the affair last?" questioned one.

"It's not over yet," he answered. "Next question."

That got a laugh.

"Why didn't you get married back then?"

"I figured if she was going to marry one of the more infamous bachelors in the western hemisphere, I needed to clean up my act. Otherwise, she might have sued me for defamation of character."

"Do you love him?" Meg was asked.

Her smile was radiant. "Yes."

"Jack, do you love her?"

He whispered in Meg's ear. They kissed, making it last by making it sweet. Shutters flashed. "That's not an answer," someone complained.

"Yes, I love her," he replied.

For some obscure reason, that famous picture of Charles and Diana resplendent in their wedding clothes, kissing on the balcony of Buckingham Palace entered his mind.

Was that what he was in for? This one shining moment of shared and studied romance, shown to the masses, then left to wither into a slow and very public demise?

In the slenderness of the fingers that were interlocked with his, he felt her conviction. Did he dare let it in? Did he dare allow himself to feel his own?

Katie called to say she was hungry. Meg announced it was time for them to go in. He regretted leaving the cameras. He'd never been less sure of what the media would make of such an impromptu performance.

That's when he realized his problem. It wasn't a performance.

He made some feeble excuse to Meg and left her and Katie at the door of the house. He couldn't bring himself to go inside. He didn't want to disappoint them. He didn't want to disappoint himself. What was happening to him? Before, he had always been able to read the tabloids and find out.

He headed for east wing and noticed the strangest things. Like the grain of the grass, stamped in crisscrosses by the groundskeeper who mowed it. And the breeze that was high enough to rustle only the tops of the tallest trees.

Garbage littered the street where the media had camped. The news satellite truck was gone. Some diehards remained. They were the worst ones, the ones he recognized from his long practice in the art of avoidance.

There was one in particular whom Jack had actually sued for following him incessantly. Jack didn't recall the man's name. The suit had been won a couple of years ago. The man obeyed the judge's edict most of the time, although on days like today, it was understood that all bets were off.

Maybe that's why Jack retrieved a garbage bag from housekeeping and went out to clean up the street himself. If nothing else, he admired the man's tenacity.

The man got his wish, an exclusive scoop, though it was only in pictures. Jack didn't speak other than to greet the security guard.

It took only a few minutes to clean up the mess. He stuffed the bag half-full, went back through the gate and left the trash with the guard with orders to keep the street clean if such a mess was made again. He then waved his thanks and sent a glance toward the photographer beyond the gate.

Rick. The man's name was Rick Madsen.

The next day, when Jack saw the series of photos splashed across the front page of the newspaper, he had to admit he looked a little stiff. Katie was smiling. Meg had the most interesting expression of all. Pride radiated from her. The kind of pride a man had a duty to live up to. She deserved the very best. So did Katie. More importantly, they deserved his very best, too.

Twelve

Jack insisted that she wear her wedding gown for the silent auction they were to attend that night. Meg didn't understand why he even wanted her to go. Despite his saying he loved her quite publicly, he had yet to say it in private. And they hadn't slept together since Jack moved out of her bedroom weeks ago.

"Didn't you tell me you bought that particular gown because it could be worn again?" he asked, checking his black tie in her mirror. "It isn't strictly a wedding gown, you said."

Meg tied the belt of her robe tighter. "I can't believe you remember the conversation."

"The dress was memorable. Especially with you in it."

Though minor compared to his usual innuendos, the suggestiveness of the comment made Meg feel weary. Was that all he cared about? What she looked like? "Fine," she said. "I'll wear it."

She made sure she dressed out of sight, though. The sheerness of the gown demanded she wear undergarments that were slight in and of themselves. Seeing them outlining her curves in the mirror made her nervous. Maybe she should go to him right now and get the sex thing over with. Once they did the dreaded deed, she wouldn't have to worry about when it would happen again or how.

But she was uncertain about whether she truly was ready to commit herself, body and soul. Without the common link of their child, what bound them together?

She used to think their sexual chemistry was the mortar that cemented the foundation of their marriage, but chemistry wasn't all it was cracked up to be. It left her confused, her heart hollow. Like now. Her husband was what—ten feet away? She couldn't even bring herself to go to him for the comfort of physical release.

Her inability to confide in him only worsened her sense of isolation. They had always been honest with each other. But she didn't know what he was thinking anymore. He treated her with surprising affection, even respect, and it wasn't only in public. But the love he claimed to feel was absent. At least it felt absent to her.

She had to accept the fact that Jack simply wasn't capable of loving her the way she wanted. The love of connection and partnership existed only in her mind—the mind of an incurable romantic.

Well, she definitely was cured now. She just had to concentrate harder on the healthier parts of their

relationship. Like how wonderful he was with Katie.
And his ability to compromise. The attention he focused on them was as lavish as it was genuine. Patience had become one of his virtues. He really was
trying as hard as he could.

When she saw how good he looked in his tuxedo
it struck her again that romance was a sad thing to
lose. It would have been fun to say, Remember
when? Remember what happened when we last wore
these clothes?

Except nothing happened on their honeymoon. It
had all happened at Amanda and Bram's wedding.

Their affair had been elemental, primal. Even now,
it felt like something she'd conjured from the stuff
of fantasies. From the moment he'd whispered in her
ear, she felt different. She had acted different, too.
She had taken full advantage of the fact that she
looked far older than she was. That evening she acted
far older, too. She never felt innocent with Jack. He'd
brought out something deeper in her, something ma-
ture.

Her school chums had described how they lost
their virginity enough times for her to know what to
expect. She may not have experienced everything,
but after five years of living on her own abroad, she
certainly wasn't naive. The fear of the uninitiated she
hid well. Jack had been a masterful teacher, even if
he didn't realize he was playing the role. She had
been that willing a student.

He was the safest man she'd ever met. Brother to
her brother's wife, he represented the forbidden. Like
most artists she'd studied, the forbidden lured the
creative with a freedom of expression all its own.

He'd made her laugh with wickedness. He made

her drink, too, both wine and the glee of his smile; she'd become drunk enough to sing, even when there was no music. The first time he kissed her, in fact, was to keep her from being too loud. He didn't want them to be overheard. That's when he opened her to a whole new world.

She'd give anything to have those days of discovery back, those days and nights she spent in a hotel room with a man spun from fantasy and her most romantic of dreams. Jack spoke to her in the language of love, and she was instantly transported to her second home. She had the veneer of the cultured and sophisticated, and she thought she knew exactly what she wanted.

She wanted to give him a night to remember, to reignite the flame that burned so passionately between them. Was that so hard? He had said he loved her, in front of all those reporters. But he'd built another wall around himself, and now she had to break through it. She could do it if she tried, if she remembered that with their wedding clothes came their wedding night. She'd ready herself over the course of the evening, and once they got home...

"Edward is bringing the car around. Are you ready?"

"Yes." She smiled at him and accepted the wrap he settled around her shoulders. He smiled, too.

"You look stunning," he said.

"Thank you."

"Shall we?"

He offered his arm. She nurtured that bit of anticipation, and put out of her mind the possibility that she was destined for heartache.

The limousine driver opened the door. She ducked

and Jack assisted, then he walked around the car to get in on the other side. It was all quite normal. On some level, though, it felt new, and she told herself that things were different now, that her love for this man and their daughter would rule her from this moment forward.

"I have a surprise," he said when he settled beside her.

"Really?" she asked neutrally, stopping the idiocy of hope that vibrated through her. She shouldn't do that to him or to herself. He'd already given her everything he was capable of. She had to make that enough.

"We've been invited to a wedding."

"Anyone I know?"

"Afraid so." She felt a sense of déjà vu when he nuzzled her ear. "I want you to be my wife."

Strangely moved by his manner, she was unable to puzzle out why. He had said these things before. "But I already am your wife."

"It's another ambush, Meg, one you can stop if you wish. Edward is completely at your disposal. Currently, he is driving us to a church. A priest will be there to conduct our wedding ceremony.

"*Our* wedding ceremony."

"He will say the same vows we took before. We'll repeat them like we did before. It's simple."

"Nobody else knows about this?"

"Edward might have an inkling. He knows we're heading for a church."

"An empty church."

"It depends on what you mean by empty. At the very least, you, me, the priest and God will be there."

She put her hand to her chest, touched the simple gold cross she wore. "Don't tease me like that."

"I'm not teasing. I'm prepared to give you my solemn vow to love you and keep you for the rest of my life."

"But we already said those vows. We're already married."

"Not before God, we're not."

"So now you're telling me you believe in God?"

"Ah, Meg," he said sighing. "You always manage to cut right to the heart of the matter."

"To stand up and lie before God is a sin, Jack. For you to suggest that I do it..." She shook her head. "I can't. I won't."

"Would it be a lie?"

"It isn't fair to ask me that question. Not when you haven't answered it yourself."

"You're right. But the real question is, will you believe what I say?"

"Of course I'll believe you—" she stopped short. He was right. She didn't believe much of anything he said anymore. Not really and truly.

She looked away and swallowed hard. Was this what happened when couples felt they had to divorce? Was it an inability to believe in each other? It was painful to look at someone you loved and know you didn't trust him.

Yet she had trusted Allen, and she hadn't been able to conjure up for him the strong feelings she had for Jack. Allen went to church with her every Sunday, too.

Was she so different? Was she any less human, any less afraid to stand before God and admit what lived in her heart?

"Why now?" she asked quietly.

"The truth is, I've been able to think clearly without the distraction of constantly putting the moves on you. I understand what I want now and what I hope to achieve. I'm ready to fight for you with everything I've got."

"But what if we don't believe in the same things?"

"What if we do?"

"We might not always. People change."

He brought her hand up and kissed the back of it. "I don't have a crystal ball. I can't see into the future anymore than you can. What I can tell you is that I've decided to look forward rather than back. Whether you want to call it God, fate or destiny, the game of life doesn't come with any guarantees. Them's the rules."

"Is everything a game to you?"

"If it is, I want you on my side. You're my ringer. You've seen the worst, you've seen the best, or will, if you join me in holy matrimony."

"That's just it. Will it be holy?"

"I promise to try. You're the one person I can't lie to. You and God. And I can't control the two of you, either. It scares the hell out of me."

"I scare you?"

He looked out the tinted window. "Sure. You might decide to turn me down. You might take Katie and leave. Even if you stay, something terrible could happen. There might be an accident. Either you or Katie could die. Much as I love you, I can't save you. I can't save anyone. I can't be my father, either."

"You want to be your father?"

He gave her a bittersweet smile. "It's a hard thing for me to face. I'm supposed to be the chosen one. I'm supposed to climb every mountain and right every wrong. When I discovered I didn't have that power, it was a rather humbling experience. I hate to lose. I decided I'd rather not be like him at all than louse it up. The last thing I wanted was to tarnish the legacy he left behind. But I have more secrets, Meg. I find them extremely hard to confess. Especially to you."

"More secrets?" She held more tightly to her cross then.

"I'm rather proud of them, actually."

"Proud?" She literally gulped. "Dare I ask why?"

"Dare I tell is the question. The hard part for me is admitting I have a good side as well as a bad side. It's easier to be bad. People don't expect much from me then. But that's about to change."

"Change how?"

"I've already instructed my assistant to send out press releases announcing what I've been up to these past few years. It's been one of my secrets, you see. Which means we'll have more than the usual crowd outside the gates tomorrow. I wanted to prepare you for that, Meg, no matter what you say about renewing our vows."

"I have to know what this secret is about?"

"Remember the foundation to promote world peace that my father started? Well, I've started a foundation as well."

"What kind?"

"A children's foundation. But I'll tell you all about that later. Right now, I don't want it to be a factor in the decision I've asked you to make. I don't want you to stand and take these vows unless you truly believe in *me*. I need to hear you say you love me for who I am, not for what I do.''

''I can't believe this is happening. You're making me cry. You should have told me to bring tissues. I'm going to look awful for my own wedding.''

''Why would you need tissues when your trusty husband always carries a handkerchief?''

He blotted her tears himself. ''Your beauty has nothing to do with the way you look, Meg. It's the way you are.''

That really got her bawling. How could he do this to her? She felt foolish and hopeful and scared. Was it real?

He kept dabbing at her face with such concern, she kissed him, and suddenly she wanted to make love right there in the car. He knew it, too. He teased her by breathing heavy and wagged a scolding finger at her, saying there was no way he was going to let her mess up his clothes.

He read her like a book. He always had. When she told him that, he let out a laugh that emanated from deep in his gut. She had never heard Jack laugh like that, deep, like he was really letting go. It leavened the tension between them. She gripped his hand.

Was there hope for them yet?

The parking lot of the church was empty and dark. It was darker inside. With only two of them, the minister didn't want to illuminate the building. He didn't want to risk drawing attention to a very public couple who desired to privately renew their vows.

Jack had thought of flowers, but not in the form of a traditional bridal bouquet. Instead, he settled a crown of white roses on her head. She pinned a matching boutonniere on his lapel.

They stood in the vestibule and tugged off their wedding bands, exchanging them for the ceremony. Jack had another secret, another gift to give, and he was nervous about his bride's response to it. He didn't fool with the black velvet box. He simply showed her the diamond ring, holding it up to sparkle in the candlelight. All he could think of to say were the simplest of words. "Will you marry me?"

"Oh, Jack." She smiled brilliantly in spite of her tears. "Yes."

She held out her hand. He steadied it and slid the ring on. "Meg, I give this ring as a symbol of my full and abiding faith that we will be truly married."

She spoke with special gravity. "I accept your ring with my full and abiding faith that we will be truly married."

He clasped her hand. "I have one more secret, Meg."

He gestured toward the shadows in the rear of the vestibule. Meg heard a girlish squeal of excitement, sweet and familiar.

Katie marched out in her flower girl best, holding Eleanor's hand. "Grandma said you'd come soon. She said we have extra-special church tonight," she announced with a great sense of importance.

"Not just church, Katie," Jack answered, holding something behind his back. "I told Grandma I wanted to tell you what was happening at church tonight myself." He presented a little basket filled with rose petals. "Your mother and I want you to be our flower girl."

"Again?"

"Again."

Katie's eyes widened. "Is this church with a wedding in it, too?"

Meg knelt to hug her. "Yes, Katie. And I'm so glad you're here to be a part of it."

Katie grabbed Jack's hand along with Meg's, putting the two together. "Mommy, you be the bride. My first daddy will be the angel in heaven and my bi'log'cal Daddy will be the prince."

Meg smoothed Katie's hair and squeezed Jack's hand. "Sweetie, I couldn't agree more."

Taking her little basket, Katie started the ceremony. Eleanor watched her from the front of the church, encouraging her on.

Candles marked every other pew and lit a path up the aisle. When the time came, Meg and Jack walked the path together, her hand tucked into the crook of his arm.

They met the priest at the foot of the altar. Katie and Eleanor stood nearby. One large unlit candle was set in the middle of the altar, while two smaller tapers were lit on either side.

Meg and Jack faced one another and, echoing the priest, spoke the same vows they had spoken before. They kissed when permission was given. The only part that was different was the lighting of the large candle in the middle of the altar.

Flame cast shadows on each of their faces as they tilted the tapers and brought them to light the wick of the marriage candle.

Once the lighting was done, they joined hands and blew out the flames, standing before the altar. Katie and Eleanor joined them and they thanked the priest, exited the church, climbed together into the limousine, and Jack told the driver to take them home.

"Katie's asleep in her own bed and we're alone in our own room, Meg," Jack said to her later that night. "No one can see us."

Meg pointed up at the ceiling of their bedroom. "He can."

Jack appeared to find that rather amusing. "He's seen us before, Meg. He's been watching all along."

She laid her hands on the shiny lapels of his tux. She wanted to think Jack's words were true. She wanted this to work, wanted to believe that consecration had the power to heal their marriage.

Jack said he wanted the same things. She wasn't sure if he believed in the same things she did, however. She searched his face and felt the warmth of his hands linked behind her, fitted to the small of her back.

If she went up on tiptoe she could reach his mouth and get them started. Kissing was easy, her mouth to his. Already her heart raced. She arched to fit her body to his. She knew what she wanted. She could feel how much he wanted it, too. They hadn't been together for a long time.

"How about we start with a dance?" he asked.

"A dance?" Disappointment assailed her.

"Remember our song, the night we first met? Sing a few bars, will you?"

He started her swaying, but the silence was heavy between them and tunes weren't what came to her mind. She started to cry.

"Hush, Meg." He hugged her close. "It's all right."

"I want it to be good," her voice broke. "Good as before."

"Only better," he whispered. "Like it means something."

She cried harder and confessed the things that weighed heavy on her mind. Like what if now wasn't great, and what if they ended up hating each other and getting divorced. Or what if they hated each other and stayed married. Or what if something happened to Katie, or to him, or to her, even.

He listened with great seriousness, as if she was talking about the Holy Grail or something. He kept rubbing her back and feeding her tissues because his handkerchief had long been saturated.

She finished finally and smeared at her tears, feeling too juvenile to even look at him. That's when he scooped her up and carried her to the bed.

He laid her down and lay beside her, fully dressed, though he flipped off his shoes. "What am I going to do with you, Meg?"

"Love me?"

"Aside from that."

She got serious then. "Tolerate my insecurities."

"I'm glad to hear you have them."

She looked at him askance.

"In case by some miracle you hadn't noticed, I'm not perfect, either."

"Newsflash. Jack Tarkenton admits to imperfection."

"You bet I do. It's not easy living up to a man who is the paragon of the universe."

"It's not easy being a work of art."

"I think I'm beginning to understand the forces underway here."

Made easier by this foray into humor, she decided to be bold. She put her hand on the front of his trousers. "I'm ready. How about you?"

"Now, Meg. I'm trying to be a good boy, a model husband, angelic in the extreme. You are making a mockery of my conversion."

"You already are good, Jack. Especially here, with me. It is sacred, what we have. It must be sacred, since it brought us together and made Katie."

He took her hand and drew it to his heart. "Ready?"

That's how they began, with her tracing the shape of a heart on his chest and burrowing her fingers between the studs he wore so she could reach his skin. Eventually, she lay open his shirt and laid down her head and listened to the thunder she found there.

He massaged the knot of nerves at the base of her neck and she melted, melted into the heat of his chest until he drew her up and they kissed for the first time since church.

This kiss was just as special.

She helped him off with his shirt. He made her stand to take off her dress, lifting it from where it pooled on the floor and hanging it for her.

Her underclothes took a much longer time. She wasn't nearly so gentle or patient with his. Fortunately, he didn't seem to mind.

Who was this man she married, the father of her child?

She lay under him and he had such a look of love in his eyes. Katie's eyes. Meg recalled the church with its stained glass windows and candlelight. Private and pretty, she couldn't imagine a better setting for such a solemn ceremony. Except maybe here, on their bed, the two of them naked before God.

The joining was a ritual, familiar and warm. They had built a foundation, a foundation that hadn't been wrong, human though it was. It carried them along and brought them to this point, this place, this moment of truth, the joining of two into one.

Trading breath, she pressed herself closer to him, heart to heart, flesh to flesh. There were no more secrets between them.

Except one. It was conceived that day, a secret to them both.

When Meg found out, Jack was at her side in their bathroom, intent on the little white stick that was supposed to turn a certain color to indicate the result of a home pregnancy test.

She really should have suggested he drink a couple of cups of coffee before helping her do this, Meg thought. "What color is it?"

"It's blue," he said, consulting the box that had held the test.

"Is that positive or negative?"

"According to the directions, it's positive. Is that good?"

She nodded. "Positive is *very* good. It means I'm pregnant."

He looked stunned. "Sit down. No, wait. Don't move. Let me get some pillows."

"Pillows?"

"Pillows and blankets. Are you sure you feel okay? I thought pregnant women threw up all the time."

Meg wanted to laugh. She didn't dare. She had never seen him this anxious, even when Katie was sick. "Pregnancy rarely makes women feel sick *all* the time. Sometimes it happens in the morning, but some women never feel sick at all. I didn't when I was carrying Katie."

"I missed that. I don't want to miss any more. Now you get back into bed and I'll bring you breakfast. You're supposed to stay off your feet, right? And where's Katie? She needs to be told. It's going to take her time to get used to the idea of having a brother or sister."

"We have quite a few months, Jack, to help her get used to the idea. I also think it might be nice if we got dressed first."

"Are you sure it's positive?" He scanned the test directions again. "Blue means we're having a baby?"

"I'm positive it is positive. You're going to be a father again."

"I never held Katie when she was a baby. What if I do it wrong?"

"You won't." The man looked so worried, Meg rose and pressed the entire length of her body against his. "As a matter of fact," she whispered brazenly into his ear, "I've never met a man who does it better than you."

"Meg, I wasn't talking about that."

"I was."

"You were?" He gripped her upper arms, holding her back. "But we can't."

"I don't know about you, buster, but I'm not going without. Not for months on end."

"Won't it hurt the baby?"

"And here I thought you knew everything there is

to know about the inner workings of a woman's body. No, Jack, making love won't hurt the baby.''

"What about you? I don't want to do anything that might hurt you.''

"Haven't you heard what happens to a woman's libido when she's pregnant? It goes sky high. She becomes insatiable.''

"Insatiable?''

"It's true,'' she said, nodding. ''At least at this moment, it's true. It would be extremely unhealthy for me to hold back.'' She walked her fingers up his chest and rose on tiptoe to kiss him.

He lifted her and settled her on the bed. ''Unhealthy, huh?'' The box that held the pregnancy test went flying. ''And here I thought I was the insatiable one in this marriage,'' he growled, nibbling her ear.

"Well, I'm going to give you a run for your money. Besides, I want to celebrate. What better way is there to celebrate having a baby than practicing to make another one?''

"Another one? I haven't even gotten used to the idea of this one yet.''

"This is just a practice, remember?''

He smiled his smuggest smile. ''You know how I love to practice.''

Afterwards, they rested side by side on the bed with her head pillowed on his shoulder. Eventually, Meg lifted her head to better see his face. ''Which do you want, Jack, a boy or a girl?''

"Funny you should ask. I was just thinking about that.''

"I thought you might be. So which is it?''

"I just want the baby to be healthy, Meg, and for

you to be all right. But what about you? Do you have a preference?"

"I've already given you a daughter. I'd like to give you a son."

A look of pain crossed his face. "I don't know. I don't know what kind of father I'd be to a son. I'm afraid I might expect too much."

"You'd be a very good father to a son, just like you are with your daughter."

He laid his hand on the side of her face. "Where do you get your faith, Meg?"

She laid her hand on the side of his face. "My faith comes from you, Jack, by way of Katie and the baby and the many people you yourself have given hope to, especially the children you've helped around the world with your foundation."

"But you didn't know about that part until later. I can't help but wonder why you even gave me a second chance. You couldn't know how it would all turn out in the end."

"I wouldn't change a moment of how we came together. I learned what love is, and what it really means. So have you. And I certainly wouldn't have you any other way."

Meg and Jack Tarkenton
Announce the Birth of Their Son
John Bertram Tarkenton III
Date of arrival: July 30 5:24 p.m.
Length: 21 inches
Weight: 7 lbs. 9 oz.

* * * * *

FORTUNE'S
Children™

**The Fortune family requests
the honor of your presence at the weddings of**

Silhouette Desire's scintillating new miniseries,
featuring the beloved Fortune family
and five of your favorite authors.

The Secretary and the Millionaire
by Leanne Banks (SD #1208, 4/99)

When handsome Jack Fortune asked his dependable assistant to
become his daughter's temporary, live-in nanny, Amanda Corbain
knew almost all her secret wishes had come true. But Amanda
had one final wish before this Cinderella assignment ended....

The Groom's Revenge
by Susan Crosby (SD #1214, 5/99)

Powerful tycoon Gray McGuire was bent on destroying the
Fortune family. Until he met sweet Mollie Shaw. And this sprightly
redhead was about to show him that the best revenge is...
falling in love!

Undercover Groom
by Merline Lovelace (SD #1220, 6/99)

Who was Mason Chandler? Chloe Fortune thought she knew
everything about her groom. But as their wedding day
approached, would his secret past destroy their love?

Available at your favorite retail outlet.

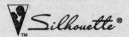

If you enjoyed what you just read,
then we've got an offer you can't resist!

Take 2 bestselling
love stories FREE!
Plus get a FREE surprise gift!

Clip this page and mail it to Silhouette Reader Service™

IN U.S.A.	IN CANADA
3010 Walden Ave.	P.O. Box 609
P.O. Box 1867	Fort Erie, Ontario
Buffalo, N.Y. 14240-1867	L2A 5X3

YES! Please send me 2 free Silhouette Desire® novels and my free surprise gift. Then send me 6 brand-new novels every month, which I will receive months before they're available in stores. In the U.S.A., bill me at the bargain price of $3.12 plus 25¢ delivery per book and applicable sales tax, if any*. In Canada, bill me at the bargain price of $3.49 plus 25¢ delivery per book and applicable taxes**. That's the complete price and a savings of over 10% off the cover prices—what a great deal! I understand that accepting the 2 free books and gift places me under no obligation ever to buy any books. I can always return a shipment and cancel at any time. Even if I never buy another book from Silhouette, the 2 free books and gift are mine to keep forever. So why not take us up on our invitation. You'll be glad you did!

225 SEN CNFA
326 SEN CNFC

Name	(PLEASE PRINT)	
Address	Apt.#	
City	State/Prov.	Zip/Postal Code

* Terms and prices subject to change without notice. Sales tax applicable in N.Y.
** Canadian residents will be charged applicable provincial taxes and GST.
  All orders subject to approval. Offer limited to one per household.
  ® are registered trademarks of Harlequin Enterprises Limited.

SILHOUETTE® Desire®

MAN of the Month

May '99
LOVE ME TRUE
#1213 by ANN MAJOR

June '99
THE STARDUST COWBOY
#1219 by Anne McAllister

July '99
PRINCE CHARMING'S CHILD
#1225 by Jennifer Greene

August '99
THAT BOSS OF MINE
#1231 by Elizabeth Bevarly

September '99
LEAN, MEAN & LONESOME
#1237 by Annette Broadrick

October '99
FOREVER FLINT
#1243 by Barbara Boswell

MAN OF THE MONTH

For ten years Silhouette Desire
has been giving readers the ultimate in sexy,
irresistible heroes. Come join the celebration as some
of your favorite authors help celebrate our
anniversary with the most sensual, emotional love
stories ever!

Available at your favorite retail outlet.

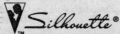

Coming in June 1999 from

Silhouette Books...

Those matchmaking folks at Gulliver's Travels are at it again—and look who they're working their magic on this time, in

HOLIDAY *Honeymoons*

Two Tickets to Paradise

For the first time anywhere, enjoy these two new complete stories in one sizzling volume!

HIS FIRST FATHER'S DAY   **Merline Lovelace**
A little girl's search for her father leads her to Tony Peretti's front door...and leads *Tony* into the arms of his long-lost love—the child's mother!

MARRIED ON THE FOURTH   **Carole Buck**
Can summer love turn into the real thing? When it comes to Maddy Malone and Evan Blake's Independence Day romance, the answer is a definite "yes!"

Don't miss this brand-new release—
HOLIDAY HONEYMOONS: Two Tickets to Paradise—
coming June 1999, only from Silhouette Books.

Available at your favorite retail outlet.

COMING NEXT MONTH

#1219 THE STARDUST COWBOY—Anne McAllister
Man of the Month/Code of the West
Seductive cowboy Riley Stratton claimed he had given up on happily-ever-after, but that didn't stop Dori Malone. When she and her son inherited half of the Stratton ranch, she was determined to show Riley that all of his forgotten dreams could come true...but only with her!

#1220 UNDERCOVER GROOM—Merline Lovelace
Fortune's Children: The Brides
Falling in love with her pretend fiancé was not part of Chloe Fortune's plan. But when she found out that he had a secret life, she fled. Now Mason Chandler was out to catch his runaway bride—and convince her that the only place to run was straight into his arms.

#1221 BELOVED SHEIKH—Alexandra Sellers
Sons of the Desert
One moment Zara was about to be kissed by handsome Sheikh Rafi, in the next she was kidnapped! And her captor was a dead ringer for the prince. Whom could she trust? Then "Rafi" appeared with a plan of rescue and a promise to make her queen. Was this a trap...or the only way back into the arms of her beloved sheikh?

#1222 ONE SMALL SECRET—Meagan McKinney
After nine years, Mark Griffin was back in town and playing havoc with Honor Shaw's emotions. Honor had never forgotten the summer she had spent in Mark's arms—and he wanted to pick up where they had left off. But would he still desire her once he learned her secret?

#1223 TAMING TALL, DARK BRANDON—Joan Elliott Pickart
The Bachelor Bet
Confirmed bachelor Brandon Hamilton had long ago given up on the idea of home, hearth and babies. But when he met stubborn beauty Andrea Cunningham, he found himself in danger of being thoroughly and irrevocably tamed....

#1224 THE WILLFUL WIFE—Suzanne Simms
Mathis Hazard didn't want anything to do with Desiree Stratford, but he couldn't turn his back on her need for protection. He agreed to help her as long as she followed *his* rules. But watching over Desiree each day—and night—had Mathis wondering if he was the one in danger...of losing his heart.